Privacation

Privacation

A novel by

J. Hayes Hurley

ISBN 978-1-257-85529-2

Croesus Books

To Ron and Pat

Cover art: "Warehouse of the Infinite"
Douglas Leichter

Chapter One

She was gazing at Mark with what he took to be frank disgust. What was it? Had he not shaved properly? Was his suit inappropriate? Was he committing an unforgivable gaffe this instant? Roasting away in the caldron of her eyes, he sat huddled in his chair like a snotty child playing hide and seek within the confines of his own fantasy life where beauty and wonder danced for him alone, stupidly assuming she ought to applaud that and call it noble, or at least clever. She did not. Her gaze told him she would rather cut off her chubby right hand than to go on interviewing a client armed with nothing but an appalling lack of insight, and even less polish. There was no hope for it. He dared invite guilt on top of shame by moving his eyes from her gaze.

The walls of her office were painted robin's egg blue as in a David Lynch nightmare. On the one to his right was hung a glossy photo of her exchanging deep eye contact with Sally Jesse Raphael. Quietly panicking, Mark met her gaze again, humbly aware that he was on the defensive side of her massive, lavender, lacquered desk and that from all indications, and despite the fact that he *had* provided for his adult place in the world, he still did not have a clue, did not "get it" and never would, and this despite his being over fifty years old. What was it, the sudden onset of mental sloppiness, or was it an ongoing, galloping naïveté he brought to this office, calling it his creative life? She went on gazing and, finally, she spoke to him.

"I don't know what you expect, Dr. Forrest, but our services are what they are from our end. I wonder if you are up to reacting to them in a sufficient manner so as to do yourself any good within your own pre-set financial limits."

"I gave you ten thousand dollars, Ms Caraway. That should be proof enough that I am … that I want it."

She gazed the more, dissolving his defenses as if with mental acid, her redesigned eyebrows now slightly raised and he thought, *I do grasp, on the intellectual surface of it at least, that one need not like the other person if it is strictly a business relationship but still ... why does she have to dye her hair the color of egg yolks and don face powder like she was applying military camouflage and ... what is that dress she is wearing; is it a tent? That coral-colored rose stitched into it is, at the least, the size of her entire amorphous abdomen.*

"I am Ms. Foss, Dr. Forrest! My mother is Ms. Caraway."

"Oh, I thought … but didn't I retain…?"

"For ten thousand! My mother consents to take a writer on for no less than four thousand dollars a week and with a sixteen week minimum. You are lucky I am able to juggle some lighter assignments so that ... never mind. Let me ask you this, Dr. Forrest, do you understand what this is all about? This is the real book world you have stumbled into. You want sales you have to pay for them!"

"Sales? I never said sales. I want readers who…"

Both of her overly manicured hands came up like a pair of road signs saying halt.

"Readers! I guarantee sales, not readers. Readers? God! I don't know anyone who actually *reads* novels anymore. It is, in today's world, positively *immoral* to spend time doing that."

She further registered her disgust with him by picking at the filed ends of the fingernails of her left hand with those of her right and said, "Just sit there a bit and try to grasp what is going on."

The desk was cut like the letter M with Ms. Foss, the power player, ensconced in the hollow on top while two other clients, both men, sat on the diagonal sides of that letter's underside. Mark Forrest was stuck on the point in the middle.

"Mr. Jaeger?"

Mr. Jaeger, the bag of bones on Mark's left, was simply ancient. His snow-white hair stood up stupidly over a forehead coated with black age spots and the while he crassly fingered his checkbook in his trembling hands as if he could cut away all middlemen and buy his way into something called literary fame. Apparently he had been waiting for the opportunity to burst out.

"Whatever it costs for my memoirs to …"

"What do you expect me to do for you, Mr. Jaeger? Is there some salable aspect of your scribbling about your own life as an insurance salesman in Poland that I ought to promote?"

"I wrote a neat little piece in my book that … about my first time playing golf … about how surprised I was when the ball went straight towards the hole, and I was wondering …"

"Wondering what? How do you want me to exploit that? Do you have a hook? I surely do not see one."

"If you could use your influence to get the PGA to supply one of their promotional photos, perhaps an overhead shot from the Masters, one of the wide-angled color shots with all the flowers in bloom and the grass neatly mowed, a photo that would bring out the … golf atmosphere I so neatly capture in my memoir."

Ms. Foss did not bother to gaze witheringly at the old man, whose ego now reverberated through the halls of fleeting fame, though doing so unnoticed, as does the fifth element.

"You sit there as well, Mr. Jaeger. All of you sit there. My mother needs me for a moment. There is coffee if you must have it but don't spill it on the desk, please."

She got up and left the room, her flower-covered figure dancing back and forth between the merely large and the immense. At once the man on Mark's right gave him one of those dreaded public smiles.

"I admire you, Dr. Forrest."

"Me? Did you read any of my novels?"

"Read you? No, not really. But I couldn't help overhearing what you said to Ms. Foss when you first sat down."

Mark stared at the man, who hastened to add, "I am Jerry Stevens, best seller."

"What did I say?"

"That you actually write fiction without a contract."

"But don't … if you are a writer … don't you write? Don't writers write? I mean, I do my work, make my living, and then I write."

Stevens repeated the onslaught by continuing to push his public, professional grin into the air. He was dressed in an expensive business suit and a pink power tie and, unlike Mark Forrest, the serious fiction writer, or Mr. Jaeger, the flat-out vanity writer, he quite obviously knew his way about offices like this one.

"On the contrary. I never touch a keyboard before I have a contract in hand."

"You talk to these people all the time?"

"Talk to them? I virtually live with them. It takes years sometimes. I lunch with my agent twice a week here in Manhattan. Eventually we work up a commercial concept and then we go to lunch with editors. There the concept becomes re-conceptualized. We work as a committee. We monitor trends. We anticipate what the public is going to be reading or what we feel we can cajole them into reading, using my original concept as a starter but keeping in mind that novel writing is a democratic process the soul of which involves continuous compromise. Eventually we give our findings over to a larger panel at a publishing house that is attuned to the most dominant cultural crosscurrents. There the real excitement begins. Plots change from day to day, joke writers are hired, and fine-tuning is employed so that book buyers will not be challenged or made to feel uncomfortable. When it is finally clear to all of us that we have a possible winner, I sign a contract and go down into the well for ten to twenty weeks. Immediately afterward I join with Ms. Caraway. As a rule, that is. Alas she is punishing me this time out, by relegating me to her daughter."

"Why?"

"I showed signs of slipping in my last novel."

"Slipping?"

"My sales fell off. I am in sack cloth and ashes this moment."

"But fiction writers who … aren't you … the life is …"

That bright smile flashed again, cutting off all further dialogue.

"Like I said … I admire you. May I pour coffee for anyone?"

Ms. Foss was gone forty-five minutes. When she came back it was clear her mood had further soured and she sent Mr. Jaeger and Mr. Stevens away at once.

"Best to call me in about a month, Mr. Jaeger. Jerry? See you at Twenty One later for cocktails."

If Mark thought he was special now he had Ms. Foss to himself he was immediately disabused of that. She gazed at him and spoke frostily.

"I can only give you this one appointment, Dr. Forrest. I advise you to listen."

"I am listening."

"This is the hard and fast rule. Sales are bought. That is why you came to us whether you care to admit it or not. As to my service: I will set you up within the limits of your own check but if you do not sell that is your fault and not mine. Understood?"

"I just think I am a fine writer and I want …"

"Don't bring up that word 'readers' again. Do you hear?"

"Yes … ma'am."

Ms. Foss took time to light a narrow, low-tar cigarette and to let the smoke escape through her nostrils and into the air like two blue snakes into still water. She was obviously bored in the extreme.

"Promoting male writers who do not have their finger on power concepts is growing increasingly more difficult. The Feminists wrecked everything. Women are the only ones still buying fiction books in significant numbers and they have fallen into the habit, as an unthinking mass, of assuming that male writers must talk to them on their terms. Here at Caraway we struggle against this, though, admittedly, we sometimes try to repackage male writers to make them more sensitive to their insensitive female readers. With you, Dr. Forrest, there will be no makeover. There is no use."

"Good. No. I mean, I just write and… say … where exactly is my money to go?"

"I will book you into a few bookstore signings and I will put in requests for you to appear on some standard media outlets. I will compile the list and mail it to you. Your job is to show up and to promote yourself. Any questions?"

"That is it?"

"For ten thousand, yes. Now I must call this session to an end."

"But what about … aren't you going to tell them that I write serious literature and…"

"Tch. Tch. *Dr.* Forrest. That is another word that I forbid you to use."

"What word?"

"Literature. 'Literature' and 'readers' are words forbidden to you. Think, instead, as a writer, of gaining sales in the real book world. In the real book world books are commodities, like potatoes or leaf blowers. The farmer who sells only thirteen potatoes is a failure. Can you grasp that?"

He tried, but before he could succeed was interrupted with,

"Not here, Dr. Forrest! Grasp it elsewhere. Good-bye. I will send you your list."

Mark found himself back on Vanderbilt Avenue a minute later where the cold wind added further insult to his person. Pulling his overcoat collar up over his ears his thoughts turned petulant.

"Doesn't she appreciate that I am being conspired against?"

There was something to this.

His publisher, Ryan Salter, of Salter and Salter, the only company he had ever dealt with had, six months ago, informed him that his latest novel, *Bleak,* was going to be printed and placed in the distributor's warehouse, and that was that. There were to be no advertisements and no publicity campaign coming from Salter and

Salter. Once more Ryan informed him that the publishing house's legal responsibilities to him had been fulfilled to the letter.

"Look at your contract if you don't believe us."

Mark didn't get it, though eventually there came the consequences regardless. Used to sales topping one hundred and fifty copies per novel, something that allowed him to daydream of literary genius, cult status, and of Belles-lettres immortality within the canon, he found out that he had sold exactly thirteen copies of *Bleak* in the six-month period since its release. His present royalties, royalties being something he had never bothered with or about, he made his living as an internist with patient privileges at New York Hospital, did surprise him nonetheless; he got a check for just under nine dollars, considerably off his usual rake-in of close to one hundred dollars. At once he rebelled for the sake of his art.

"The wider public deserves to read me," he declared.

"Why?" Ms. Foss had challenged.

"Well, because … I do serious writing."

"My dear Dr. Forrest, that is just why they do not read you."

Seated at a table in the Algonquin bar shivering from the cold he had just fled, Mark ordered a gin and tonic and, with a twinkle in his eye, and with a playful tone in his voice, asked his waiter, "Let me know when Dorothy Parker comes in, will you?"

The man peered down at him, frowning incomprehensively. Sighing, Mark consoled himself by removing a copy of *Bleak* from the wide, inner pocket of his black overcoat.

"It is my best work," he whispered.

Bleak referred to the aesthetic landscape he'd described early on in the novel. It was, in his judgment, a prime example of unfettered literary talent on parade. It was a masterful, multi-level presentation, it was the undifferentiated, Pythagorean stuff differentiated. His sentences in the first chapter were designed to over-stimulate readers and to cause images to explode in their imagination. Yet for the discerning reader these images, like so many cheap drawings that shriveled up when tossed upon a fire, soon faded before the hard arrangement of words on the page, and there came that moment when one could almost locate aesthetics, once and for all, right there. So his readers had the privilege of his insight. Then again he could not by definition be looking for just any readers but only those who were able to appreciate …

"The bitch says I can't say 'readers'."

Of course Mark knew better than to lay out the aesthetic alone. No novel is composed of pure aesthetics even though his hero managed to come close to operating completely within that lofty realm. There had to be a story, a story transformed into a plot, and for this Mark was as good a story man as anyone who wrote. For proof, had he not turned down multiple offers from television, and from Hollywood? He had. He put in his fifty hours a week at his medical practice on First Avenue, his "day job" as he called it, and on top of that he put in his thirty hours a week, writing. Doing the story was the craft side of novel writing; doing the aesthetic was the art side of it. Such a dichotomy held firm in Mark's mind. His drink arrived. The waiter, with dead-eyed seriousness, informed him, "I asked at the desk. We have no one named Parker staying in the hotel."

"Thank you."

Mark sipped his drink and read *Bleak.*

The novel opened with the hero, Slattery, attending a convention of money managers at the Camelback Resort in Scottsdale, Arizona. Slattery was not a money manager, his wife was. He was on vacation; that is, he was in her way from breakfast through dinner speeches, daily. He was told, "Do something with the spouses, why don't you? I am busy."

He settled for lounging at poolside, drinking rum cocktails and working on his sunburn. Cynthia Howard, wife of a Chicago money manager, a heavy-set woman with a strong voice, sat with him on the second afternoon and he found her reasonable and pleasant. On the morning of the third day she rang his room.

"Scottsdale has simply the best shopping malls in the southwest, Rich. I have a car. Let's do them."

"Oh, no, I beg you. Shopping malls … no."

"Rich! I promise it will be fun for you."

He thought. "Cynthia seems a right sort. I will trust her."

"I guess I can come," he said.

"Eleven sharp."

When the valet drove her Cadillac up to the entrance at eleven sharp, Cynthia, gave out in her strong, loud, firm, voice, "You're the man, Rich. You sit up front. Ladies? The back seat holds three."

Three overripe prunes, middle-aged women with suffering faces, appeared from out of nowhere, and they looked at Slattery as if he was an ax murderer. That was the last direct gaze they were to give him; it was clear to everyone that his presence made them uncomfortable in the extreme. Driving along moments later Cynthia set the radio on elevator music and when Mark tried to change the station she froze him with her index finger.

"We cannot have anything intrusive."

They did the first two malls following Cynthia's instructions; they coordinated their watches in front of Victoria's Secret and met back there again in forty-five minutes. Slattery spent his minutes pacing; he hated shopping, especially in enclosed malls. He could not breathe. He had assumed there would be sightseeing interspersed with … he was wrong.

The third mall was a monster. Cynthia, growing stronger in her leadership role by the minute, held complete charge over the prunes.

"We can allow two whole hours here, ladies. Though first I suggest lunch. They have a Great Crepe chain restaurant here. Shall we?"

Stuck in the back by pointed ferns, nauseated by pastel colors, his tailbone sore from sitting on a thin wooden seat, and with no place to put his elbows around the table, Slattery remained mute through the whole lunch. There were no cheeseburgers on the menu; he had to make do with a "wrap."

Cynthia directed the conversation, probing the prunes on relevant topics … like thread count in sheets. The real drama began when she announced, "I work out of the home as a teacher's aid. And you, ladies?"

It was as if she had insisted the three remove their tops in front of Slattery. They had trouble swallowing. They bowed their heads in humiliation. Two of the ladies admitted they had never worked out of the home, the third said she had once done so, part time.

"At Macy's, during the Christmas rush. It was in dinnerware."

No one asked Slattery anything. The check came and he was determined to grab it and slap down his credit card just to be out of there but … alas … Cynthia grabbed it first and began the painstaking task of reading every item they had ordered and asking, of each, what was theirs.

"I have my calculator," one of the prunes said.

She produced it. Slattery sat in wonder while she did her figuring though, the while, he wondered what she *was* figuring. Finally the calculating prune announced her results.

"The tip, not taken with the taxes added in, comes to fifteen percent of the total food and beverage bill. If we were to say … as a fiction … that we all had the same meal, then, each of us must come up with one fifth of seven dollars and eighty-nine cents. Let me calculate that next."

It was not to be. A second prune, ashen colored, had her calculator out and it was now a case of dueling calculators.

"We cannot … I will not be so spendthrift. I, for one, had no beverage. What we have to do is calculate all five bills separately and figure out the appropriate tips per person from that."

The three turned to Cynthia. Slattery looked at her as well. He could not believe how much she had taken him in after a few rum drinks by the pool.

"We will take a vote," Cynthia decided.

Cynthia and two of the prunes voted for the second pay plan. Once again no one looked at Slattery, who was tempted to raise his hand with his middle finger sticking out of it.

Of course this plan proved unwieldy. Three of the five tips, those of the prunes, came out on the odd penny and that provoked a violent, dig-in-your-heels fight. The one who had not had a beverage said she was being overcharged on purpose and the others grew sullen.

"We really ought to get shopping," Cynthia said. She was unflappable.

Writhing in Slattery's presence, the prunes began paying up, though for revenge, they rummaged about in their pocketbooks for what seemed like days, drawing out a nickel here, a dime there. The closer they got to their total, the more defeated and red-faced they became. At last it was over and they were standing before Victoria's Secret.

"Two hours it is, girls!" Cynthia sang out in her strong voice. "Good hunting!"

Slattery was suffocating. He could not bear to do two more hours of pacing, nor could he bear sitting with those hordes of defeated husbands on faux-leather couches in the waiting pit. He would die. Casting about desperately he spied an employee heading down an unmarked, narrow corridor between two giant department spaces. Without hesitation he followed. The employee eventually opened a door on the left side marked "employees only" but Slattery kept on walking until he arrived at a blank white door with a metal fire bar across it. There were no visible alarm warnings. He could not breathe. He pushed the bar.

At once he was in the bleak world. Rising above him was the outside rear wall of the mall, a white concrete flatness presented without a thought given to texture. It was interrupted by standpipes pockmarked by grey water damage, naked spotlights, blunt metal doors, and steel loading ramps with metal rollers and thick steel supports rammed into a filthy-surfaced spread of asphalt gone, on its uneven surface, from black to an uncertain, chalky syrup where truck bodies sat like ancient ruins. Steps away from this began the infinite spread of grey desert sand. The sky overhead was of a color that could only be described as "not blue" that surrounded an oppressive dome of stark white sunlight. What shadows there were came in tones of dirty grey.

Slattery was attracted, repulsed. This bleak world he had stepped into was …what? This bleak aesthetic world was to be accepted as not-beauty while, at the same time, it was not to be defined by the contrary of beauty, ugliness. Yet if it was not ugly, what was it? It was the bleak aesthetic.

It was foundational. Filled with the pain of this discovery, yet ecstatic that he had escaped the mall, Slattery knew at once that the world was a multiplicity within a deeper oneness, a world within which niceties like conventional beauty are, ultimately, to be understood as so much divisive fluff.

He was reminded of hot, dry Sicilian landscapes he had driven over in years past. They were stark, and bleak, yet aesthetically pleasing. Now, standing on the edge of the undeveloped desert, he was taking bleakness to its logical extreme.

There followed, in the novel, four dense pages of description. The question was, did this added analysis contribute to the growth of Slattery, the character, or was it in fact the intrusive work of Forrest, the novelist? Were these pages of self-indulgence or did they represent the deep passage of true insight. Of a sudden Forrest the novelist was returned to himself at the Algonquin. He was still furious with that Foss person but taking it out on himself.

"Ten thousand dollars!"

By four that same afternoon Mark was back in his junior two apartment on the nineteenth floor of a nondescript, 1950's red brick apartment building on East Sixty-seventh Street. His mood had not improved, he was now blaming himself for the sins of others, and more than that he could not, this day, turn off the flow of impotent rage that no matter how childish he knew it to be was going to play itself out within his being regardless. The brief hiatus he had enjoyed at the Algonquin had not lasted; he found his own rooms depressing. Casting about for alternatives, he grabbed his keys and rode the elevator down to the ground floor, entering his medical office.

"Mark? What are you doing here? Is there an emergency?"

"Afternoon, Janie. I just … I don't know. I will look at paperwork."

Janie, his kindly, pug-nosed, bushy-haired gal Friday, his longest serving and most loyal employee, who had her self-declared, solitary duties to perform on Wednesdays, gave him a motherly look, and what was, no doubt, a loving look as well. Mark pretended not to notice. He was barely of medium height, with small hands and feet, eyes that were all but transparent, and with a mop of brown hair that had not thinned with the passage of the years.

"If you really mean to pitch in, there is quite a stack of it on your desk."

"I am sure there is."

It was Wednesday, his day off. As a rule he never, ever came into the office save for emergencies. He broke that rule fewer than half a dozen times a year and only when he was feeling as ridiculous as he did today. He looked at the papers, all from insurance carriers looking to deny claims or parts of claims, calmed his self a bit and whispered, "Crap."

If he got much of it out of the way this afternoon he would have a better day tomorrow, when too many patients would be crammed into his waiting room. He sat, skimmed this paper or that, signed a few, crumbled many, and as he slipped into an enjoyably dull routine his mind took him back over the very reason he was here in the first place. It was, as he was in the habit of admitting to himself ad nauseum, a rather uplifting and mature story at that.

Mark had decided to become a novelist at age eight. At age twelve he had formulated a good thesis and a bad thesis about that decision. The good thesis was that he knew of nothing that gave the sort of sustained happiness that reading literature did and he wanted to give back to his fellow human beings the very enjoyment he got. The bad thesis was that he was not going to be a famous athlete, and writing would be his revenge. He went to high school and college and began to write and to starve. Oh, that the world thwarted his plans was awful, awful. His parents tore their hair, his girlfriend left him, and, though he stuck it out, he was sick and tired of living in single rooms and working dead end jobs. One day, and miraculously, he saw the problem for what it was.

"It is not that I have to give up writing. It is that I have to secure the proper means of support in order to do continue."

Not one budding writer in a thousand understood this as clearly as Mark Forrest did at age twenty-six. It was then, with a clear head, that he left the uncertainties of temporary employment to "bone up on his sciences" to get accepted into medical school. He did this without giving up his deeper artistic purpose in life. Now, at the age of fifty-two, he ran a satisfying if not very lucrative medical practice, one that becalmed him and granted him personal and social dignity, that allowed him to care for patients and they for him. He had as well published three novels that were the stuff of his life. It was the publication of his third novel, *Bleak,* that started this present trouble.

"Why did I ever allow myself an ego move? Am I as crass as that old fool, Mr. Jaeger? Am I as mercenary as that grinning Jerry Stevens? God, no! I should have insisted they give my book away. They could have left one copy off at every upscale bed and breakfast across America. They could have passed them out to literature classes. To hell with sales: damn Ms. Fat Foss, and hurray for serious fiction writing! Ten thousand dollars! How obscene is that? For that amount of money one can get to stay in the hospital for at least three days provided one has minimum insurance coverage for backup and there are no surgical considerations."

More insurance papers confronted him, more tangled webs of co-pay drudgery and petty office detail and then, without knowing why, he put this stack aside and reached for some lab reports that had just arrived in his office. The one on top referred to Mrs. Johanna Murphy, a brave and perky patient of Mark's, a thirty-year old woman who had just given birth to her third child.

"God bless us all."

He just couldn't believe what he read.

"We both thought it was … but … she has *that type* of cancer."

Mark put the report down and, as he always did when moved and saddened like this, he thought about the use, the sense, the bald-face excuses one made for the pure aesthetic when good women like Johanna Murphy are certainly going to die of cancer within four months leaving a husband and three children behind. What could he do as a creative writer when there was nothing he could do as a doctor? Was it enough to report incidents like this in a novel, creating characters like Virginia Woolf did Richard Dalloway, and letting his voice question the ultimate good of the artist in a world where human beings starve and suffer and need political guidance? Was it enough to say he had his "day job" on top of his serious writing? He pushed himself away from the desk and telephoned Johanna, asking her to come into his office at once. While he was waiting for her he phoned Carrie and they agreed to meet at a watering hole in TriBeCa at eight p.m. and to think about dinner, or not, from there.

Chapter Two

Some days later Mark sat gripping his knees in the "green room" of the A. C. Cottonwood news and talk show at the headquarters of the network studio in mid-Manhattan. This was fearsome Foss's doing; booking him onto the one media venue he hated on principle, television, and, not only that, but onto the show of the one media personality he particularly hated right down into his guts, A. C. Cottonwood. The "A. C. do see" hour, as his despicable fans had it, was really no different in kind from other shows merging hard news with entertainment as the new, watered-down network standard. What they offered the viewing public were pseudo-concepts called "segments", wherein fuzzy, suggestive, interactively friendly half-notions applied to entities that did not really exist, but were only suggested by suppressed quantification, were tossed out on the air, thereby allowing viewers to feel connected while they were being manipulated, and to gain the false consciousness that they were human beings alive by definition, but only so long as they kept glued to the tube.

"What do Americans think about themselves?"

"Are women happier now that they are empowered?"

"Is faith fashionable?"

A. C.'s show added the usual mini-touches called in-depth looks, dealing with such topics as teenage pregnancy or prescription drug dependence, dashing through these in thirty second sound bites stuffed between advertisements for sex products and prescription drugs, and with the studio audiences groaning their ethical approval or disapproval on cue. What made Mark so furious with A. C. Cottonwood in particular was his prissiness, his telegraphing to anyone who happened to be watching who was at all perceptive that he, A. C., was "getting down" with his viewers while remaining ever superior to them the while. The man never hid his deeper concerns with ratings and revenue streams; the overarching, sneering truth seeping through was that viewers were dumb, and that fact was making him rich. As well, A. C., with his slim-as-a-boy build, his pixie hair cut, and his precious manner, was more concerned with being hip than intelligent, again something taken to be a media standard, though he was intelligent in the way flippant, exploitive people invariably are when they sell the very souls they never believed they have. So of course he was more concerned with image than substance. This last point drove Mark over the edge. A. C. was, and at the behest of his producers, maddeningly attentive to and fearful of the short attention spans of his viewers, all of who, he knew, had the power of the clicker lying erect between their knees.

A.C. managed to hold his show together by a constant rush of trivia, interspersed with short bursts of hard news. He went from five-second references to shooting wars to the campy coverage of some rock star's plastic surgery. Like his colleagues on every channel and on any network, A. C. asked questions of guests and then impatiently cut them off before they could answer, intuiting correctly that the show was really all about him. He indulged in the usual media feeding frenzies when it came to scandal or gossip, and he played to his profiled audiences, people made mentally numb thanks to their exposure to popular ideology. He fed viewers both sides of advocacy questions and then let them vote for the winner, calling that truth. He thrived on fallacious arguments that media types called "spin" and, worst of all, he promised that the hot topic of the day was coming right up, then followed this with a series of advertisements, came back to promise that the hot topic was coming right up, followed by more advertisements, ad nauseum.

Mark waited while A. C. interviewed a woman weightlifter, a middle-Eastern terrorist expert predicting the end of western world dominance, and the ex-boyfriend of a female rock star who had poured whisky over his head at an airport check in and then let her pet poodle lick him. All of a sudden it was Mark's turn to promote his novel, *Bleak.*

A. C. greeted the novelist and bade him sit down on the couch. Yet before returning to his own seat he gave a wink to the audience, as if to say … help me through this next minute.

"Yeah, so all right, tell me … you wrote this novel about … what is it … about the back of some shopping center? Gee, if do hope you made the hero of your book a developer, Mark?"

"The shopping center scene is used to introduce an aesthetic principle that most people…"

"Whoa! That word is too intellectual for American viewers, Mark. You mean to say that *Bleak* is a good read, right? You read that book Senator Pearl wrote, about murder in the Capital building? That was a good read. Decapitations. That was some description writing."

"I do seri … I write professional fiction."

"Isn't the novel dead, Mark? I mean, Dickens would not have bothered to write all those wordy descriptions in this age; it would be a waste of time. The camera can catch the sense of scene in one pan, thus saving any of us having to plow through the fine print. Really, Mark, isn't it true that the novel has given way to the movies?"

"We are not considering …"

"I can't even tell you when last time I read a novel. I think it was the adventures of Tom Finn or … did I get that right?"

"No, you …"

"Let me hold up your book for the camera, Mark. There it … can they see that out there? I guess there's glare from the dust cover. You thought about using matt? There it is, ladies and gentlemen, *Bleak!* You know when I was at Harvard we had to read this book about masturbation. Can you beat that? Ha-ha. And you know what was on the cover? I can't say. Oprah? Where are you when I need you? Mark! Thanks a lot. This thing is available at stores isn't it? It weighs enough. If I were you I'd think about switching to a books on tape version. OK. When we come back … infidelity among today's service sector workers. Stay tuned."

"It wasn't that bad, Mark. Really, no, really, you are just being paranoid. You did fine."

Carrie Singleterry rubbed the back of Mark's neat left hand with her generous right hand while they sat at a table in the window of a restaurant called Taste of Sicily on Second Avenue that same evening. He was feeling so raw he could scarcely breathe without crying out in pain.

"If humiliation is the price behind the price, then I am so sorry I gave that woman ten thousand dollars. I should tell Ryan to give the books away. He can remainder them if he likes."

"He may do that anyway."

Mark looked up at Carrie from his plate of *pollo* and marinara sauce with a violent jerk of his head, as if becoming aware of her independent existence for the first time that evening. Carrie just smiled back at him with a show of infinite patience. She was thirty-five years old, her hair was still honey blonde and her olive toned skin still smooth; her face was full and rounded like the moon, her nose as small as a walnut, her blue eyes revealed an intelligence devoted to patience when dealing with men. She invariably wore sweaters whenever they were out together, layers of wool or cotton that accentuated her full bust in particular, while exaggerating the voluptuousness of her figure in general.

"I know that," Mark said without bothering to disguise his hurt. "I am always remaindered. It happens to be a reality in the book writing business, in case you haven't noticed."

"Now, now! Don't take your anger out on me, darling."

"I am sorry."

"You will go through your promotion schedule and that will be that. It was your choice."

"Even if I sold thousands of books I would not make enough in royalties to re-coop my ten thousand dollar investment with a publicity agent."

"Mark! This is tiresome. Quit it! Hear? You are an adult. You made a choice. "Take some responsibility."

"I'm sorry."

They finished their meal and went on to his apartment where he emptied his dishwasher and opened a bottle of red wine while she changed the linens on his bed. They met again in the sitting room where, after just one glass of wine, they abandoned that room for the bedroom, undressed in unison and climbed into bed like an old married couple.

"You want to read, Carrie?"

"I do not."

"You want to make love?"

"Do you need to ask? Do I need to ask?"

"Well, no, it is just…"

"We can if you want."

They passed on making love and nestled into their own places in the bed but were unable to sleep.

"I guess we are a New York couple," Mark said softly and Carrie sighed.

"Mark? Do you have to make that observation every single time we get together?"

"Right. Sorry."

Lying there, their bodies barely touching, Mark vowed to bite his tongue. He had finished medical school at thirty, and his residency in internal medicine at age thirty-three. He married Mattie, a gorgeous girl from Idaho, in the first year of his practice. He worked long hours and spent the remainder of his waking time writing his novels. Mattie, at first willing to be his backup, his support, his uncomplaining woman at home, grew increasingly sick of playing this dreary role, and yet she did not have the educational background to establish her independence in the big city. She was not accomplished enough as a typist to be an executive secretary, and was not willing to train herself for some rigorous profession. She left Mark after six years of marriage and went back to Idaho. She was not bitter. She had decided that she wanted open spaces. They had produced no children.

Mark suffered the loss of his wife though not for long. He met Carrie within a year, and while they dated one another exclusively for the past dozen years, neither one was willing to give up his or her own Manhattan residence. Carrie lived on the west side in a prestigious albeit dark and dingy pre-war building, Mark on the east side in his featureless utilitarian place with bad furniture. He continued to spent virtually all his hours writing and practicing medicine, she spent as many hours a week as a buyer for a major department store in the city and was gone for weeks at a time on buying trips.

When Carrie was in Manhattan they met every other night for dinner and she spent three nights a week at his place. Their relationship was, on balance, arguably pragmatic. Mark and Carrie were mature enough to know that there is no such thing as perfection in anything in this life, be it in relationships, or in medicine, or in clothes buying, or in the writing of the novel. They were beyond questioning whether or not they were happy; they had one another and they had their independence, too. They were committed career people and felt this was implicit in being a New York couple. If one of them were to exercise the option of exploring the dating scene it was not the business of the other one to know about it much less to complain if they did find out. For all that, they were potential candidates for an A. C. Cottonwood "couples segment" though Mark, for one, would have cut off his fingers rather than admit it. He touched Carrie's arm.

"You want more wine, darling?"

"I suppose."

Mark got out of bed, retrieved the bottle of red wine and grabbed two fresh glasses. They lay side by side once more, sipping good Merlot and eventually got around to allowing an habitual pattern to unfold. Mark would talk about his formative days, as a novelist, and

Carrie, who knew all his stories, would ply him with relevant questions. In this role she was better for him than Mattie ever was, for she had the patience of the present, while Mattie had been fixated on an open future.

"You were a sensitive boy, Mark."

"Yes, I … yes."

She went on and on with the usual comments, yet of late this sort of ego massaging was falling flat and actually doing harm in an odd way. It was one thing to prop up the emotions of a twenty something year old writer in the making, it was quite something else to indulge a fifty-two year old man who had three novels published and no success to show for it. In fact they were both embarrassed by Mark's willingness to indulge in self-pity. At times like this he felt like someone who was unable to give up eating fat foods or smoking cigarettes and who wanted a shoulder to cry on when what was called for was tough love. Carrie did what he asked of her, but the net result was that it left her feeling cool.

The following day proved exhausting. There was a lineup waiting for flu shots. He was behind reading lab results for dozens of patients. Mr. Montoya's PSA test was not that alarming yet he would not leave the office until Mark explained to him the entire end game to do with the male sex organ. Miss Carter had shingles and would not stop screaming. Johanna Murphy dropped by again; she was given another full hour's sympathy consult. Two detail men got by the receptionist and it took Janie fifteen minutes to remove them from his presence. There were three large patient bills unexpectedly refused by the same insurance carrier, and he had to waste an hour and a half pleading on behalf of a heart patient who could not afford his medication.

The afternoon proved even more frantic. Cancer, strokes, heart attacks, these were the hard realities. Ingrown toenails, warts, hypochondriacally projected growths, sore backs, and age spots on the back of a lady's hand, these were the lesser realities. In between came the juggling of proper insulin amounts, the occasional knee drainage, and countless treatments for the living and the not yet dead. On yet another scramble between rooms he thought, "This is what I want despite the difficulty and the exhaustion."

"Mark?"

"Yes, Janie?"

"You forgot to get a urine sample from Mr. Jarrit."

"Oh, boy."

An hour later, while examining Pricilla Moody, who had imaginary lumps in her left breast (last month it was imaginary lumps in her right breast), Mark was struck by the injustice to which all human endeavors are subjected to in the course of time. Important things, meaningful projects, and the ostensible quest for truth, beauty, and goodness, have to compete with the more trivial details of the day, minute by minute so that…

"Damn!"

He had already made that observation and had written it down at the age of fifteen.

Coming back to his apartment that evening to get ready to meet Carrie for supper, and so tired on his feet he could scarcely walk straight, for he got up at five a.m. every morning to do his serious fiction writing, Mark asked himself, "What does Carrie get out of all this?"

Chapter Three

Heading down to the Javits Center by taxi for his next, Foss-generated publicity something-or-other for his dollars, Mark, though he fought against it, began suffering a familiar sort of distaste. He wondered whether it was the case that he was right and the rest of the world wrong, or whether he was merely too arrogant for his own good when it came to hard realities of salesmanship.

In Mark's mind the process of promoting books and movies was a sickening one, a process falsely inducing people to lay out money for something they not only knew little about, but were given the wrong information about into the bargain. Instead of letting serious art bubble to the surface from the ground of aesthetics, or else come floating down from Yonder, books and movies were treated like natural products instead, like potatoes or leaf blowers as the Foss had it, and so it was that the economic bottom line trumped the aesthetic at every turn. That Mark found this wrong was his strength as an artist and his weakness as a man of the world.

Mark only read novels that were talked about by colleagues. He waited to see movies at least a year after they were first released. As a serious novelist he was right to do this, yet he had to concede that if it was up to him all writers and moviemakers would starve.

"But that is why we bow to the means of support!"

There happened to be on lower Broadway a used book store featuring best sellers going back one hundred years. When he walked through this store Mark's intuition was reinforced. Stripped of their publicity clippings, the overwhelming majority of these books were exposed in this time and place as being lifeless piles of words. That they were once best sellers had everything to do with selling and nothing to do with artistic content.

"Yet here I am, in my fifties, being my own promoter."

"Here you go, buddy, the main entrance. Ten fifty."

What Foss had booked him into was a convention of dentists. They had a cocktail party scheduled in a large ballroom at a certain hour and there they were going to rub shoulders with “authors”. The word Mark had not picked up on, even when reading his instructions, was “authors” in the plural.

Minutes later he was standing in a crowd of tooth men and their wives. He had been instructed to introduce himself to these people. Indeed he wore a name tag indicating that he was an author and had deposited a pile of his books in an adjoining foyer, but at the last moment he found himself tongue-tied and besides, his name tag was so small no one noticed what it said. The crowd took him for a lady-dentist’s spouse and he wandered about holding a gin and tonic and saying nothing to anyone and having nothing said to him. He was about to leave when his attention was drawn to a fellow “author”, a heavyset woman who was working the crowd in a manner that would make Ms. Foss proud. Fascinated and repulsed at once, Mark found himself following this woman about at a discrete distance while she worked the dentists.

The “author”, a gastroenterologist and psychologist named Sally Finkelstein, was promoting her latest diet book for women but with a twist. She argued, in this book as she did in all nine of her previous diet books, that women should learn to love themselves, meaning they should learn to adjust to their own body weight reality and stop chasing thinner models she called “unrealistic ideals.” Thus it was that several things were being accomplished with the sale of this particular diet book at once. For Sally there were sales. For the women buying her diet book there was the double satisfaction in knowing they were doing something about their fat selves while not really doing anything at all. They were eating what they wanted while readjusting their self images to what they really were. They were fat but that was OK because they were now grown comfortable with their own body images.

Mark was astounded at how well this worked. Women all over the ballroom were dissolving in tears, hugging one another, and running out into the foyer to buy Sally’s book. Meantime the men, the dentists, were gathering in tight knots to talk about the difficult patients, namely those patients who had failed to undergo root canal treatment and had gone into unbearable pain instead. Of a sudden someone with very good eyes spoke up.

“Say! Doctor Finkelstein! Here is one of your fellow authors. What is the name? Mark Forrest. What do you write, Mr. Forrest?”

“Novels, I …”

Interrupted in mid-sales pitch, Sally Finkelstein wheeled about on her generous legs and fixed Mark with a hostile look that, he admitted at once, was more than equal to that of the dreaded Foss. Whatever lingering ideas Mark might have had about "working the room" vanished in a moment; he would never be up to such a task.

Sally's gaze froze not only Mark but all the women she was talking to and the nearest knot of dentist's as well. Finally, all eyes turned to the novelist. He had to say something! As in a trance, he turned to the staring dentists and blurted out the following.

"I am one of those root canal failures. I went for root canal and about five minutes in the dentist struck some nerves and I experienced pain so unbearable I leaped up out of the chair and began circling that chair bent over like Groucho Marx while the dentist's nurse chased me round and round demanding immediate payment. He wrote me a pain prescription and they wouldn't let me go fulfill it until I turned over my Master Card for payment on the spot and when I finally got to the pharmacy I had to circle the stacks while it was being prepared and then I was outside on Second Avenue and started across but the pain was too much and I clawed open the vial to swallow the medication on the spot but the pills spilled all over the asphalt and at the same moment the light changed and the traffic came on but I went down on my knees in the middle of Second Avenue scrambling to pick up the pills because the idea of being run over by a taxi was as nothing compared to the need to stop the pain and … oh … yes … I wrote a novel called *Bleak* and if you have no intention of reading it then for Christ's sake don't bother to buy it."

He left the Javits Center knowing there would be a complaining call into the Foss. He had not packed up his box of books in the foyer; there had been so many judging eyes starting at him that he thought of nothing but fleeing. Technically the books belonged not to him but to Salter and Salter, so chances were that he would eventually have to end up paying for all of them himself.

"I paid ten thousand dollars for the privilege of buying my own work."

He did not take a taxi but wandered off through the dark streets of Manhattan on foot. His zigzag path led him along Eighth Avenue into the theater district. Here memories of his early writing ventures came back to him: times when he exhausted himself walking through the tenderloin, thinking himself existential. He tried to think this way once again but it finally dawned on him there was something wrong.

“They have sanitized the goddamn place!”

It was true. Mark Forrest’s artistic inner life was routed, this time by wholesome Disneyland fare, bland family restaurants, and by blocks of innocuous businesses.

“It is enough to make me wish for the return of toothache.”

Carrie was out of town on a buying trip to India and Thailand and would be gone from Manhattan for at least three weeks. Mark did not let this upset his routine. He got up early every day and wrote, then went to his practice, and then after dining alone went back to his apartment and to sleep. On this botched night he was too upset to go home and walking was doing him no good, so he crossed over to the east side and ducked into a nondescript bar on Third Avenue. Here the atmosphere was subdued and the clientele was mixed; a mélange of young and old, locals and out-of-towners, and all with their heads bent, indicating they were more interested in drinking than talking, which suited the novelist just fine. When a seat opened up at the bar he grabbed it.

“Gin and tonic.”

Two of these pale cocktails later Mark finally relaxed and dropped the rigid pose he was keeping on his stool. The crowd shifted around him. Eventually four young ladies pushed their way toward the single empty stool on his left and for the next five minutes were busy ordering their drinks and shouting hilariously. It was as if they brought a sea change with them. Soon the whole bar became lively. One of the four young women kept inadvertently pressing her back into Mark’s left arm and at one point she wheeled about to apologize.

“Sorry. No room.”

“It’s OK,” he answered, smiling.

She turned her attention back to her girl friends but then turned back to Mark and held out the hand holding her drink.

“Cheers. I’m Jill Cartwright.”

“Cheers. Mark Forrest.”

Hearing his name Jill stared at him, and then gave out a sound that was half laugh, half surprise.

“What do you do, Mark Forrest?”

“Do? I … I am an internist.”

At this Jill’s entire body signaled an unmistakable note of disappointment. She was no more than twenty-five years old, with close-cropped black hair, starkly bold blue eyes that looked as big as half dollars, a rather large, wandering nose stuck between two tight cheeks stretched even tighter over her wide cheekbones, and, to complete her face, a pair of absurdly thin ears sticking out through her hair on both sides of her head. She was altogether too thin, her clingy black dress accentuating the angular lines of her body like a small glove drawn over a large hand. Despite her obvious and mysterious disappointment with Mark being a physician, she could not repress the spontaneous puffs of laughter that would escape from her every few seconds.

"A doctor, huh. For a second there I thought you were … someone else."

"Another guy named Mark Forrest?"

"Yes."

"What does that one do?"

"He's my favorite novelist."

Mark, still smarting a bit from the evils of self-promotion, dropped his eyes to his drink and sat on his stool like a statue. Jill gave it another two seconds and returned her attention to her girl friends, who were exchanging banter now with some newly arrived yuppies in business suits who were holding drinks in one hand and their polished brief cases in the other. One of these men was in Mark's opinion too, too loud and, worse, he soon had his arm around Jill's shoulder and was shouting questions at her.

"Ya been to Southampton? What about Block?"

Jill answered him between her characteristic puffs of laughter It struck Mark that she was not enjoying herself. He waited until loudmouth was busy ordering more drinks and he tapped Jill on the shoulder.

"Yeah?"

"Hi … I … I ought to let you know. I am Mark Forrest the novelist."

This time Jill looked long and hard in Mark's eyes and when this stare went on and on, he mumbled, "I wrote two novels back a few years. And lately … ah … *Bleak.*"

She continued to bore in on him until, and finally, a big smile lit up her face.

"My God! You're Slattery!"

"No, no, I am … Slattery is my character. I am the author of the novel."

Jill brushed that fine distinction aside with a wide grin and leaned in very close. The yuppie tried to pull her away that moment but she warded him off. She resettled her body on her stool so that she was nearly resting against Mark. She was all smiles and angles, she was bursting with energy, and she if she had an agenda it was an irresistible one for sure.

"Forget it. You are Slattery. I know you inside out."

"You actually read the novel?"

"Of course. I read all three of your novels. *Bleak* is my favorite."

"You never know," Mark said in a half whisper.

"Let me tell you, Slattery, you are floundering around in a world of your own and you need to break out of it."

"What world is that?"

"A world wherein men are gentle and women are either too inhibited to bother with … the 'prunes' as you call them … or else too rapacious for your comfort. You need to level the sexes off, Slattery. Give your male characters a stretch and allow your female characters to settle in the middle. Flesh them out; make them real."

"Well, I…"

"Where are all the aggressive men? The Marines, the football players, the class bullies, the business tycoons, the cruel husbands, why, reading your work you would think that all boys were as sensitive as the brush strokes of Vermeer. Artists *are* sensitive to be sure, but they can raise hell as well."

"Perhaps you are right but … this is fiction. I have to be selective."

"Not good enough, Slattery. Face it. Come on now … you are afraid of women."

Hearing this old saw Mark pulled back into his world-weary physician role and eyed this perceptive young woman with what he hoped was a warning look.

"Please."

Jill, a fan he had run into by chance, one of the few fans of his writing he had ever met in person, was openly settling into her role as unofficial advisor, and Mark had the oddest feeling that there was to be no going back for either of them.

"Listen to me, Slattery. I can cure you of your self-imposed limitations. I will cure you in fact; just wait and see."

Jill grabbed his left arm in both of hers and when the yuppie tried, once again, to wrest her away Mark stood up and shouted in his face, "Get away from my woman or I'll shove your briefcase down your throat."

The man backed off and Mark's heart gave a leap. He swore there was new life pumping through his veins, and that the surge was, somehow, passing through Jill's veins as well. He lost all sense of his old self. The girl's arms tightened around his and she drew her face so close her lips were virtually brushing his cheek.

"What are you up to, Slattery?" she whispered.

Mark, who expected the high, heart-pounding feeling to go on and on, felt his earlier depression return instead. He did not want to burden this girl the way he did Carrie. He did not want to exploit his feeling sorry for himself, though he went ahead and did just that. Over the next few minutes he blurted out all his troubles with the Foss, with pre-paid publicity events, and with his *congenital* inability to promote his own books. He ended this self-pitying tirade with a frank confession of arrogance.

"I have this aesthetic sense and … I guess … most everyone else in the world does not."

Jill listened and the puffs of laughter that followed disconcerted Mark a bit. He feared he had made a fool of himself. But the girl clung to his arm and her lips stayed next to his cheek and she rubbed the back of his neck in mock sympathy and promised him this.

"You are wrong, of course, Slattery. You too readily juxtapose the wasteland of television with your novel writing, but you ignore the fact that most educated people feel the same way you do. You are avoiding competition in your own field. You'll get it right yet, Slattery, thanks to me," she bragged.

"You?"

"Why not me? Tell you what. Next time you go on one of your proscribed publicity outings I will come with you. I will be your guide, your muse, your fresh-faced hope."

"You will?"

"I volunteer, Slattery."

"Well, I think that …"

"Now, now, now. You need a woman like me to run interference for you, Slattery. You need someone like me to act as buffer between your creative self and your public self. You need to hang out with someone willing to take on the role as the Foss's alter ego."

"Maybe you are right."

"I know I am right. I am getting my doctorate in literature at N.Y.U. and know all about quiet authors like you, Slattery. You are one of those men who are oh-so-sensitive that you mistakenly think you do not fit into the harsh world where you hurl your words."

"You are studying me in a doctoral program?"

"Not formally. I mean I can't; you are not dead yet. But I do bring your name and your work up to the attention of my professors."

"What do they think of me?"

"Well, they haven't read you. Yet."

"I see."

"By the way, before I go ahead and accompany you, Slattery, tell me this. Do you have a wife stashed away somewhere?"

"I have an ex-wife in Idaho."

"And?"

"I have a kind of long term understanding with a women who is currently in India and Thailand. We are, ah, New York types. I mean … we are …"

"I got it. You have a kind of open, non-marriage."

"Technically, I am as free as a bird."

"Yeah right. I will give you my cell phone number anyway. You call me in a few days."

Chapter Four

There was a postcard from Carrie to do with curry, but there was no response from Jill to the four messages Mark left on her cell phone answering service. There was another, dreaded, publicity arrangement coming due, this one involving Mark speaking to a group of female students at, of all places, New York University, something that had escaped his conscious attention at the bar the night he met Jill. A fifth call to Jill, belatedly detailing this coincidence, went unanswered. Mark was finally ready to give her up as a pipedream. He went to the university event by himself but when he walked in the door of the conference room there was Jill.

"Hi Slattery. Glad you could make it. Throw your shoulders back, you look like a little old man on his way to have his toenails cut."

There were some fifty or more coed undergraduates and a handful of coed graduate students including Jill, who now wrapped both her arms around Mark's left arm in her familiar and possessive way, acting as if she and he had been in continuous communication all this while.

"How come you haven't answered my calls?" he whispered while she led him to the dais.

"India and Thailand might object."

"But I … need you."

"I want you to be a big boy and do your duty on your own. Now, get ready to get up there and when you do, try to act like a literary lion, OK?"

It was Jill who introduced him. It came to light that she had contacted the Foss and got permission run interference here, though in her further preliminary comments she left the students with the impression that Mark Forrest was certainly a man steeped in literary merit who was enjoying the very thing he wanted most in life, to have his work speak for him.

He started in. He gave a detailed explanation of the bleak aesthetic, his voice rarely wavering, his tone soft and gentle. When he finished, to polite but not thundering applause, it was Jill who stepped forward to field questions for him.

There was no hostile attack. Questions were mostly to do with how these young women viewed possible sexual relations between their own self-projections and the book's main character, Slattery. This ordeal of pleasantness was over in an hour, not counting an additional forty minutes of wine and cheese, and he was thankful that Jill kept him the more firmly in tow while he spoke to several of the students one on one during this session.

The girls he talked to promised to read his book but without promising to buy his book. Mark, forgetting that he was here to sell books, fully approved of the their stance. He, too, felt that right-thinking people more or less expected to be given a book by an author they met personally and to be given that book as a gift. The mutual understanding was that if they were hustled, if they were pressured into buying the thing, then the author could not be a very good writer to being with, but must be selling the equivalent of potatoes or leaf blowers. It was only afterwards when Jill was putting her coat on and Mark was standing around hoping she would be going off with him that she informed him that he had in fact sold five copies of *Bleak* that evening. Mark was tight-lipped but Jill was not.

"You don't get much for your ten thousand. Too bad you had to pay the Foss the whole amount up front."

"Let's not talk about it. Are you … are we going out now?"

She looked at Mark for a long moment. During that frightful passage of time he was convinced she was not going out with him. Finally her puff of laughter broke through.

"Listen to me, Slattery. I am a student of serious literature. I am not one of those women who mix up their admiration for a writer with the fuzzy idea they have to somehow physically reward him."

"I did. I didn't … look. I just…"

"Shut up, Slattery. I'll go out with you."

"You will?"

She laughed.

"You older guys are a gas. In your day you put a macho face on things and the women went along. Today, women push your buttons and *then* they go along. It comes to the same thing in the end, Slattery. So stop worrying."

He took her to an out of the way jazz club in the East Village called Jules. They sat at a tiny table in a very dark corner of an already dark room. Once seated they were both too shy to speak and it entered his head that, at last, neither he nor Jill were role playing any longer and that they might just be able to communicate on some meaningful level. The only problem was what was the content of that communication to be? It was Jill who was to select it. She played it safe.

"So, Slattery, you faced a group of contemporary females tonight. What do you think?"

"You were right. They were not prunes, nor were they rapacious demons."

"So I win. I have induced you to eliminate some of your cherished clichés. What else?"

"Huh?"

"How *do* you find the younger, liberated, post-Feminist generation of women?"

He let his eyes roam over her stick-thin body, smiled, and said, "For starters, I find them too fleshy."

"I beg your pardon?"

He leaned forward and spoke to Jill with their noses literally touching.

"It must be the growth hormones in the meat they eat. Eighteen year old girls are taller, denser … fleshier. It is disconcerting."

Jill laughed, letting it out in little puffs.

"What else, Slattery?"

"They are vulgar. The audience tonight being an exception, of course."

"Hmmm."

"They equate being free with swearing and shouting in public. They feel it is their right to exude loudness. They flaunt the very idea of getting away with outrageous behavior."

"They can and they do just that. Cut them some slack, Slattery. They are convinced they are just escaping from some Victorian social prison. Let the ideology unwind. It won't last."

"Yes, but that leaves them victims of determinism."

"What do you want them to do, Slattery, set forth in a neat mass to become aesthetically sensitive novelists like you?"

"God forbid. Well, at least they can be readers."

"What else?"

"Sports!"

"Come again?"

"Did you happen to notice how many of these young women were wearing sports team jackets? What are they here in college to do, to play soccer, basketball, volleyball, softball, and …"

"You want them all to go to afternoon teas and then come out on Saturday afternoon in their Camelhair coats to cheer on the boys?"

"I guess I do."

"Forget it. What else?"

Before he let this one loose Mark's eyes frantically searched Jill's arms.

"Tattoos. They are all tattooed."

"Young women do go in for that. You are right."

"I miss the traditional feminine roles."

"Gentle men and retiring women. Mark, you are so damn retro."

"I am not singling out today's young women. Our entire culture is fallen, it … when I was on the A. C. Cottonwood show I … it was hideous."

"His show is bad, I agree with you."

"You do?"

Their noses were still touching and hers was larger than his. Jill brought her hands up, held Mark by his cheeks, leaned forward, and gave him a kiss.

"There. Gentle man. And let me not forget … you are a doctor as well."

"I am that."

"Tell you what. I am not about to let that sensitive, serious, aesthetically intoxicated novelist have his way with me. On the other hand, doctor, I am going to ask you to give me a thorough examination … tonight."

They went to Jill's place, a boldly painted, graduate student-housing studio in the immediate neighborhood of N. Y. U. As soon as he was let inside and had his coat off, Mark got busy, as authors will do, in trying to spot his novels amongst the hundred or so books stuffed onto the bookshelves. Jill noticed this at once.

"I traded in your three books for a small pepperoni pizza."

"Oh."

"Well, it did have double cheese."

"Hmmm."

"Here! Here. Here they are."

They were not on the bookshelf but were lying in a stack of three on the foot of her bed. She picked them up, one at a time, and rubbed them against his left temple as a joke, then proceeded to undress him.

Half an hour later she was holding him in her thin arms and he was speaking to her about his talent. He was trying, the while, not to equate his talent with his gentleness. He ran on and on, as he did with Carrie, calling up anything and everything that came to mind. When he started repeating himself regarding aesthetics Jill gave him a squeeze.

"You said all that in your book, Slattery. You spelled it out very plainly. I *got* it."

"Did I say all that? I don't think…"

"Give me some credit, Slattery. I am not a prune, I am not a rapacious Foss, and I understand your concerns as well as you do. Your sense of the aesthetic is rather conventional by the way and, if I must say so, old hat."

"Sorry, I … yes."

"Worse, you don't trust people who know about literature but do not choose to write it, right?"

"Ah… Well. People who …"

"People like me you mean? People in academe or in publishing unsettle you. You want to relegate us to the mass but we won't go trundling off there for you. You pull your autoimmune trick and we still cling to you. You cannot hide in your own consciousness any more."

"Well, I …"

"Am I good in bed, Slattery?"

"Huh? Are you kidding?"

"This women you live with without living with her, is she good in bed?"

"Come on, Jill. Stop it."

"Tell me the truth, Slattery. What are you feeling right now?"

"You want to know?"

"I do."

"I like women who hold me once in a while and who listen to me and comfort me and allow me to spill me guts. I like it when they know what I am going to say ahead of time and then smoothly step in to keep the story going and who…"

"Let me guess. Your woman … what is her name?"

"Carrie Singleterry."

"Carrie is no different than me. She plays the same role I am playing right this instant, right?"

"I confess."

"Are you that much of a cad, Slattery?"

"I feel guilty as hell if that is what you want me to say. But I do not care."

Jill pulled his ears and when the air came puffing out of her lips she was busy rolling her big eyes, too.

"You are a phony at bottom, Slattery. Admit it. Pretending to be routed and in full flight when the Foss's of this world come along, while, all the while, you are manipulating a careful selection of this world's women to serve you in bed and to stroke your ego, too. You have no problem with career women, Slattery. In fact you like it when they are off doing what they have to do. It gives you time to write your novels and to see your patients. It is just that, when you do get together with your women, you like them to flatter you the way a nurse fluffs up a patient's bed. You get away with that just because it is the way you ply your charm."

"You are tearing me apart, Jill."

"No, Slattery. I am calling your bluff. You say you feel guilty? Really? You handle your guilt well. You are bedding Carrie Singleterry and Jill Cartwright at the same time. Isn't that right, Slattery?"

"Jill, don't."

"Don't what?"

"Don't be a Foss with a soft voice."

Jill laughed in little puffs and, with another series of deliberate moves, resettled herself back in the circle of his arms again. The tweaking of the male conscience was over, as was the concocted or forced or automatic tea and sympathy bit. It was on to the real fight.

"How old is Carrie?"

"Thirty-five."

"Seventeen years your junior."

"Yes."

"What about me?"

"Subtract another decade."

"Are you a Don Juan, Slattery? Do you comb the city looking for women like me?"

"Hardly."

"Yes you do! I bet you do! You are a sneaky one in any case. You are a male of the worse sort. You are a Don Juan hiding behind a mask of sensitivity. Why, instead of having some Leporello count your conquests, you insist that your conquests excuse you from having to admit to a list."

"Well."

"No wonder you have no room in your books for Marines and football players. You do better than they do! You score more than they do!"

"Carrie! Ah … Jill!"

"Caught you."

"I apologize."

"Too late, Slattery. You are going to have to start making up your mind pretty soon."

"You or … Carrie?"

"How perceptive of you."

Mark said nothing but Jill did not let him rest.

"Or do you think you can juggle both of us, Slattery?"

"Well, she is out of town a lot and …"

"Slattery! I don't have to jump in bed with a man your age. You're no statue of David, you know."

"Granted."

"On the other hand I am here, festering under your skin whether you want to admit it or not. I am *just like* your familiar Carrie; I listen to you and I hold you when the time comes for you to … well up … and when you are busy with your work I dutifully go off to mine."

"You are precocious."

"I am that. Do you think you are the only novelist I read and admire?"

"No, but, I would hope I am the only one you bed."

"Keep it up, Slattery. I warn you."

"Jill. I …"

"Shhh. Quit while you are ahead."

"Mrs. Howell? Doreen? What you have is a slight cold. It will be gone in a week. You do not have esophageal cancer."

"But my sister …"

"It was awful about Betty. But you are not Betty and you do not have what she had."

Mrs. Howell was both relieved and disturbed at once: she was relieved that she was not going to die the same horrid death her sister did; she was disturbed now that Mark had taken away her latest hypochondriacally inadequate defense. She would go home healthy but already suffering "the shift". The cancer she did not have but feared above all else would shift and slide from her esophagus to her arm pit. She would call for another doctor's appointment. When Mark examined her arm pit and found it sound, the cancer would move into her wrist, or her vagina, or her stomach. Mark would counsel her like a doting father and she would be calm for a time, though the faux-cancer would show up again in her spine. Mark would, once again, insist she seek psychiatric help but she would bristle at this. For the next ten appointments with him she would be the soul of common sense and hard-bitten reality. She was one of his longest-standing patients.

He got her out of the office and busied himself treating two brothers, twins, who had contracted gonorrhea with the same woman, who insisted on coming in to see Mark together, and who started bickering with one another when Mark asked them certain probing questions. As he refereed this weary squabble he smiled inwardly. He had to play the role of the mature professional and was doing it well, while at the same time Jill's precocious take on him hovered about his consciousness with prickling but scarcely wounding irony. He felt like a marriage counselor skillfully saving some couple's marriage while his own was in tatters.

Another dozen patients followed the twins and when he took a frantic moment to fill out paper work between examinations, Janie, ever kindly and bushy-haired, came straight over to lend her help.

"I can fill in most of this stuff for you, Mark."

"No, I better…"

"I don't mind."

"Janie, you are already overworked as it is and …"

"I want to do it, Mark. I don't mind. I can fill in all but your signature and then line them up so you can just wiggle the pen without even lifting the pages."

"Janie, you are too kind."

He lifted his hand as if he was going to pat her on the back but did not. His inward smile expanded itself into a leer. He thought, "Do not play that game with Janie."

Carrie was still away. There was something about an Asian silk crisis and a side trip to Malaysia and though this was not the first time her buying trips had been extended it was upsetting Mark and for reasons he cared not to delve into that deeply.

Yet he knew why. Carrie was away but he had not seen Jill since the night they spent in her studio. Once again Jill was proving to be extraordinarily good at playing hard to get and just when his other woman was unavailable. Of course it would be crass of him to play one woman off against the other at his convenience. He certainly did not want to do that, and yet it was not his doing that Carrie was staying away. Worse, he was suffering all the complications of having two women to juggle even though neither the one nor the other was available. The damage was being done in his mind, not out in the spacetime of Manhattan. He felt through all of this like a non-bottle alcoholic does when, with nothing intoxicating coursing through his veins, he nonetheless trots himself through cycles of guilt and rage.

"I *am* juggling two women, both of them exemplary characters, and I am left feeling like a monster. And all this while being left all by myself."

Which was, he further noted, no better, psychologically, than what was happening to Mrs. Doreen Howell. He was the one punishing himself and for what reason? Carrie had made it plain and had stated it often enough: if he wanted to date another women it was his business. If she wanted to date another man that was her business. They were … yes … he knew the party line.

The office shut down for the day but Mark stayed on, fighting the losing battle against paper work. Janie worked by his side.

"Janie, go home."

"It is nothing. I'll stay."

Janie lived in Pelham with her widowed mother and two Siamese cats. She did not date and she rarely ventured into Manhattan on her days off. She had, and with the cooperation of Dr. Mark Forrest, developed an extraordinarily nuanced approach to her job; she was not a person with strong social defenses, she did not go through her day keeping people at arm's length for her own safety, though she was selective regardless.

They worked so closely Janie's hair tickled Mark's cheeks every few seconds. It was too much for him; he felt stifled. He was living inside out of late and, thank God he added as an afterthought, he was finding it somewhat funny.

"Janie? I am calling it a day. I am going. See? I am walking towards the door. You stay if you want. I suggest you go home."

Mark had drawn the line and it was not the first time he had drawn the line and no doubt it would not be the last. Janie was ready to jump into his arms but only with the expectation that they would soon be married. He did not want that. Furthermore, and over against what Jill had said, he was no Don Juan. He did not collect female scalps. He *was* a responsible male. He was a consummate professional. He would not cross any lines with his employees and he would not allow himself to be dragged down into any sensual morass.

Closing the door behind him and heading towards his apartment, Mark gave a laugh.

"I find it funny that I am so pragmatic. I am the possessor of the pure aesthetic as a novelist. I am a noble physician. I have the tacit go-ahead by Carrie to pursue ladies on the side, but the overt order by Jill to chose one lady or the other. I am free; I am as predictable as one of Pavlov's dogs."

He opened a can of tuna fish for dinner and, as the crunch of the can opener sounded in his ears he dutifully monitored his saliva flow.

Chapter Five

Elizabeth Dorchester, acquisitions librarian, met Mark in the foyer of the modest library of a modest township located along the Hudson River, some twenty miles north of Manhattan. It was part of the Foss's strategic plan to have Mark visit a few libraries in the region in order to convince staff to purchase his book, the Foss having called ahead to prepare the way. As Foss put it in her letter to the novelist:

"You ought never discount sales to libraries. Light a fire under these people in one region, let them get the word out, and before you know it hundreds if not thousands of copies of your book will be bought."

Elizabeth, a highly-strung woman of Mark's age, had allowed her hair to go white while simultaneously letting it grow down to her shoulders, something that suited her so long as she wore her tortoise shell glasses along with dresses with a high collar, and kept a suitable distance from everyone she encountered.

"Hello! Dr. Forrest is it? I am Mrs. Dorchester. Good of you to visit us."

"Hello, Mrs. Dorchester. It is my pleasure to come here. I have been here before, you know."

"Oh, really?

"Yes, I once, as a kind of hobby, visited dozens of small town libraries in this corner of the world marveling at the architecture, the furnishings, and the way these buildings lend themselves to the preservation of our literary culture."

This statement, meant to be flattering, disconcerted Elizabeth and she stumbled a bit leading him into the main reading room. Mark, who remembered this place well, was looking forward to seeing its grand reading room with its oriental rugs and leather chairs, its tasteful, quiet corners, and its lovingly preserved devotion to such vaunted American authors as Hawthorne, Hemmingway, and Howells. What he saw upon his return stopped him dead.

"What in the name of God have you done to this library, Madam?"

"What do you mean?"

"These … changes!"

"Oh, sir, we have updated our library to meet our patrons changing needs."

Mark stared at the "update", feeling sick inside. The old reading room was torn apart; several dozen cheap computers, sitting on laminated computer tables, were crowed into what once was the most gracious seating area Mark could remember. Stacks of lurid magazines were stuffed into the crannies and there were at least ten teenagers busy manipulating their game boys and causing electronic ejaculations to occur in beeps and buzzers. Stacks of DVD's rose up where oriental rugs once hung. Where there had been an original Turner now hung a warning about sexual harassment, a current list of books on tape, and a call for volunteers for the Boys and Girls Club of America.

Worse, it was unrelentingly noisy in this debased space. Noise, something that Mark could not conceive of as being associated with a library, permeated every corner of the room. Elizabeth, proud of having keep pace with the popular culture, grew disconcerted over Mark's reaction. He managed to curtail further comment with a heroic reigning in of his emotions and whispered, "May I see the stacks?"

As he remembered them, the late Eighteenth Century stacks area was a white-washed wonder with tiny staircases leading to this cubby or that, and with clusters of wooden chairs set around carefully crafted tables.

"Of course. This way."

"Oh, my God."

The stacks were still there but they were, literally, reduced by half. In place of what was ripped away were more computers! Worse again, there was a hideous addition to the original library building, one that, as he could see from the pasteboard sign announcing its contents, held the following: how to books, books on computer technology, books on women's health, books on nutrition, and a dozen more categories of books worthy of discussion on the A. C. Cottonwood show. Mark despaired all over again, took control of himself once again, then asked coolly, "Mrs. Dorchester, do tell me. What characterizes this change you have made?"

Elizabeth finally saw her duty and promptly did it.

"Dr. Forrest, I ask you to be reasonable. Libraries, today, have nothing to do with literature. Do not be confused, however. People are still literate; it is just that they use their literacy skills in other areas.

He turned to her.

"And you, Mrs. Dorchester?"

"Me? Dr. Forrest, I wouldn't think of wasting my time reading fiction. I do like to read romances before I go to sleep of course; but no one professional librarian that *I* know is willing to plow through what we used to call the novel."

Mark had learned this same lesson from the Foss. Still…

"Why did you … why was it necessary to rip out half the fiction stacks?"

"Oh, that. Under the old standard, we retained the same number of fiction shelves while we expanded the library in other ways. We merely weeded out books as we went. Every time we added new fiction books we had to remove older ones from the same shelves. But under the new standard, we expand the library for new uses while simultaneously decreasing the size of the fiction stacks. It is just the way it is, Dr. Forrest."

She led him back through the ruined reading room to the circulation module and there Mark sheepishly produced a copy of *Bleak.*

"I guess I … what I came here for, Mrs. Dorchester, was to induce you, as acquisitions librarian, to purchase this particular novel. I think Ms. Foss has called?"

Elizabeth gave him a sweet smile. She made no secret of the fact that she considered him a boob but she was not unkind at heart.

"I think that I …"

Just then a door burst open behind the circulation desk and out stepped two men. One was a dissipated older man with a scowl on his face; the other was a young man with a sneering look. Elizabeth Dorchester snapped to nervous attention.

"Oh, oh! Ah … Mr. Willoughby?"

The older man, who seemed hell bent on leaving the library as soon as possible, scarcely paused, and in obvious irritation growled, "Yeah what?"

"This is Dr. Forrest. He has come all the way from Manhattan to request that we purchase his novel, *Bleak.* Dr. Forrest, this is our head librarian, Mr. Willoughby, and his assistant, Mr. Morton. Wouldn't you know, Mr. Willoughby, Dr. Forrest happens to have with him a sample copy of his novel and …"

Willoughby, along with Morton, returned to his initial pace, ignoring Mark.

"Listen," Mark said in a loud voice. "Forget about the purchase. Let me just give you this copy."

Willoughby paused again, grasped the novel Mark shoved towards him, looked at it for one disdainful second, then shoved it back into the hands of its author."

"No thanks," he mumbled, as he and Morton went out through the foyer.

Elizabeth Dorchester's face turned beet red. Mark tried to remain calm but found it difficult to draw breath. After a few more moments of this mutual embarrassment, he mumbled his good-bye and left. He made his way through the small parking lot to where his rented car was parked. He did not notice the two men smoking cigarettes just behind it, and the two men who were standing there smoking did not notice Mark approach. The next thing Mark heard was this.

"You believe the nerve of that asshole?"

He looked up just as Willoughby did and their eyes locked into an expression of eternal and mutual hatred.

Back in the city that evening, while picking at Chinese takeout in his apartment, Mark reread, once again, a passage from his novel, *Bleak.*

"Like Henry Miller before him, who wrote it all down and called it *The Books In My Life,* Slattery, too, recalled his days growing up with books, though his was a simple reverie, one that never failed to plunge him into a state of ecstasy once removed, or what some would call a deliciously heightened nostalgia.

"We read novels. That was our pleasant and useful activity; that was our aesthetic. We never questioned it. On the contrary we lost ourselves in it and we assumed that everyone else who was alive did the same. We exhausted the children's sections of libraries and moved into adult fare, we combed the bookstores, we borrowed from one another, and when we were acquainted with the best of the best we systematically read all the works of the best. We did now and again read our books in easy chairs it is true but more often than not we lay on couches with warm Afghan rugs covering us and with cats lying on our chests and bellies. Time went by without notice save that we were trained to look up and away from the pages during natural breaks though for what reason we could never fathom. We came prepared: we had our food stacked on tables beside our couches. We munched cookies, sandwiches, soft drinks and selections of fruit; none of these items distracted us from our reading; they were no more to us than the warmth of the rugs or the soft furry bodies of the cats.

"The more we read the more we extended our reading. We read Proust straight through and, without pause, read him straight through again. We often skipped school for a week or more at a time, calling in sick and feeling better for it, for, we argued, what is better, reading a complex novel or chanting some silly lesson by rote?

"Finally, we were able to turn our sustained pleasure into virtuous activity and, of course, happiness was ours and, ultimately, we were able to merge that happiness, which was obtained by reading good fiction, with sheer contemplation. Aesthetics, ethics, and the ultimate reality of oneness were ours. We never went so far as to argue, as Epictetus did, that we ought be prepared to think without reading; for the fact of the matter was no one was looking to take away our books. That was the supreme gift of our culture!"

Mark read this, sighed, and grasped a shrimp with his chopsticks. A letter from a friend lay open on the table where he had his take out boxes. He wrote telling Mark that a good many successful, but now aging novelists were going around giving lectures these days and that they all had the same theme: *The Novel is Dead.* Apparently there was money to be made saying that. Mark talked to the air.

"Updike has appeared on television to say that he was the last of the novelists in that novelists used to be a part of a town's population just as are butchers and barbers. He was the town novelist seen wearing his tweed coat with the leather patches and smoking his pipe. Nowadays, there is no novelist to be granted such a place in space."

Talking to the air Mark added, "Say you are a novelist and people ask: 'Hmmm. But what do you do for a living?"

"I am a goddamn practicing internist, you idiot!"

Dr. Forrest met with three very sick patients one after another. All three happened to be conscientious enough to come see him after he had "turned them over to specialists" and he was thankful for that; more often than not he saw patients who were either not sick at all or who could be managed for this chronic ailment of that, only to lose them to specialists once they did become seriously ill. That was the nature of modern medicine. He followed up these consults by examining a man who was taking out a three million dollar life insurance policy. After that lengthy visit he spoke with a woman who thought her left palm was swollen though it was not.

"I was in the shower, Dr. Forrest, when I looked at my palm and it was growing."

"Look at it, Mrs. Roberts. It is the same size as your right palm. They are both of normal size."

"Oh, no, I mean … not the palm but the …here, below the thumb, along the base of my hand it … it is swelling."

"No. No. It always looks like that. It is just that it happened to catch your attention this morning is all. Nothing to worry about."

Mrs. Roberts went home immensely relieved. Mark continued to labor at the office. Hypochondria, anxiety, false self diagnosis, and the corrosive influence of drug company advertising were distractions he dealt with on a daily basis and which wore at him as much as did the excess of paper work.

"Dr.? It said on TV to ask your doctor about that pill."

"It is not for you, Mrs. Gildersleeve."

"But they said it relieves heartburn and acid reflux."

"It also places your liver at risk."

"But they said ask your doctor."

"And so you have."

"But my friend, Mary, asked her doctor and her doctor prescribed it."

"Well, I am not that doctor and you are not Mary."

"But if I want to assure myself of not having heartburn why can't I ask Mary's doctor if you won't give it to me?"

"You are free to do as you wish, Mrs. Gildersleeve."

The woman eyed Dr. Forrest, her eyes narrowed and she became visibly calculative. Mark easily imagined what she was thinking.

"This business of switching doctors is often inconvenient. So many of them are ignorant of what is being taught on television. This one, for example, who they say spends all his free time writing dumb books that nobody reads, isn't being properly educated like a New York doctor ought to be. Why, on the A. C. Cottonwood show last night they talked about this very pill? They say Dr. Forrest appeared on that show, so he ought to be better informed. What are these doctors for,

anyway? They are there to dispense the drugs we need. Why should they let their negative opinions get in the way? The drug companies are doing us a service by hooking up with the television people; now we patients know what drugs to take. There ought to be a law against people like Dr. Forrest stopping me from being cured. He just is jealous of the TV, not to mention the Internet, where we can get as much information about doctoring as he knows."

Mark finished up shortly after six in the evening and when he was shutting off the lights he came upon Janie still seated at her own desk.

"Janie, go home. The day is done. There is no more to do this evening."

Janie made no move to get up, nor did she pretend to be busy with paper work. Instead she asked, rather coldly, "Is Carrie back from her trip to Asia?"

"Yes she is. She got back at the beginning of this week. Now she is busy coordinating some spring collection or other. Busy, busy, busy, right?"

"Mark?"

"Huh?"

"Are you two having dinner together tonight?"

"No. I won't see Carrie for a while. She's … busy."

"I was thinking of dining in Manhattan this evening myself."

"Ah. Lots of choices for restaurants in this city."

Janie's face started to form a frown, one that would mask a deeper disappointment, but she caught it and turned it into a depreciating smile instead. Mark hurried through the last of his closing tasks and then held the door for Janie, who walked by him wearing her coat and looking suddenly frail and helpless.

"Get home safely, Janie," he whispered as he locked the office door and headed for the elevator.

Janie passed out of the building without answering him, her bushy hair bouncing over her coat collar.

Mark stopped at his apartment only to get his own overcoat and forty minutes later was sitting at a table at the Lion's Head having pasta and red wine with Marty McSorley who, like Mark, was both a physician and a writer of fiction. Marty and Mark were simpatico, getting together for dinner and drinks at least once a month. As they proceeded through their meal Marty, a cardiologist, held sway, complaining about his practice.

"They got me rushing my way through patients just to fill their coffers. I mean … what do they want? Ten goddamn minutes per patient? How can I do an examination in ten minutes? You are lucky you are in private practice, Mark. I am hounded to death by a health center that is only concerned about the bottom line."

"Yeah, yeah. You want to trade practices with me? You try fulfilling my paper work."

Conscious, of a sudden, that he had been grousing through the whole meal, Marty broke off with an embarrassed laugh and busied himself with his wine. He was a large, fair-haired man with a spreading belly. Mark smiled and asked, "How's your love life?"

Marty snorted.

"You know, during the last year of my marriage I went through every nurse on the night shift but one, the bitch. Now that I am officially divorced women are only willing to date me if I drag my financial portfolio along. They mean business these days. So I can tell you, I have had exactly two one-night stands over the past eighteen months or so. How about you? How's it going with Carrie?"

"Carrie and I are … I don't know … the woman is busy these days."

"It's like Seinfeld with you guys, right?"

"I think so."

"Anyone else? Have you decided what to do about your gal Friday as yet?"

"I am not going to do anything, Marty. I told you as much."

"Just kidding. Janie … I wish she would go out with me. I keep asking her but she … "

"She doesn't find you attractive."

"I know. Funny, when I was going through those nurses, looks never factored into the equation."

They let the subject drop, finished their meal, paid, left the place, and went down to TriBeCa to drink beer at one of the few remaining Westie dives. They talked about the Knicks and the Lakers, and finally Mark confided to Marty what was really on his mind.

"I met a younger woman. I say I met her even though she hardly sees me. She comes to me when she damn well feels like it, but then ignores my calls for weeks at a time."

Marty nodded his head. He was up on "younger women."

"I know that type. Liberated, independent, bristling with suspicions that you are trying to control her, and hell bent on calling the shots even if it means frustrating their own designs."

"She is all of that and yet … I like her. More than that, I'm … more than that."

"Is that the only problem, getting to see her on your time?"

"No. The thing is, she is every bit as supportive of me as Carrie is. In fact they are so much alike, these two, that it scares me."

"What's her name?"

"Jill. She's getting a doctorate in literature and she is a fan of my novels."

"Ah, ha! How much younger is she than … Carrie?"

"A lot."

"What exactly are you complaining about? You have two women."

"I don't have either one of them most nights. I am a virtual hermit. And Jill is playing hard ball."

"Telling you to choose?"

"I am afraid so."

"Watch yourself, my friend. You'll end up fat and lonely like me."

"Really?"

"I mean it. You are about to find out, as I have, that you cannot carry your creative act of writing novels into the streets of Manhattan in every moment. You constantly complain that there is a cultural wasteland out there; you need to realizie that you have to step in it now and again yourself."

"Yet there are so many realities that … I can't even keep track of them as a creative writer. I am aware of my writing and my practice, but there are revolutions going on in the world and there are poor people suffering on this earth and … I don't know what else."

"So?"

"Jill says I am too restrictive in my writing."

"What does she expect? You can't write about everything. And while we are on the subject, and sorry to bring this up when you expressly said you were not talking about it, isn't that the whole purpose of publicity? To let people in other worlds know about your world?"

"Are you saying that the Foss is right and I am wrong?"

"What do you think, Mark? Is it ever a bad thing to promote good writing? Don't you feel an obligation to let the public in on you?"

"If you put it that way."

"I do. From what you tell me, tonight, you are admitting to living in several adult worlds, and in one more world, that of aesthetics, which, though it is adult, was born in your childhood."

"Yeah, it is the childhood that …"

"Mark, once you put words down on paper and go public with them in your novels you make your creative world an adult world, too. You are not accepting responsibility for that."

"If you put it that way."

Chapter Six

Mark, pushing one shopping cart and dragging a second behind him until his wrists screamed in protest, slogged through the aisles of a giant, or, using his word "gross" discount store in New Jersey. He was led along by Jill Cartwright as she methodologically stripped shelves of selected items every few yards, tossing them in one cart or the other and reacting to Mark's stress with little puffs of laughter. She had, at last, called the novelist back this Sunday morning, informing him that if he wanted to see her he had to take her to Jersey and help her shop.

"I can't afford to shop the Manhattan boutiques. This is my semi-annual raid."

Carrie was still busy and had not been to dinner with Mark much less to his apartment for what was turning into a long stretch, so when Jill did call, Mark agreed to pick her up in an hour. He kept a car in the underground parking lot of his building and only took it out when leaving Manhattan, and it was this vehicle that they drove across the Hudson.

"You seek bargains here, Jill? It is so …"

"I know. It is a cultural wasteland."

"Yes."

"This is where America shops, Slattery. Don't you know America? Don't you care? Aren't you trying to write the great American novel?"

Mark looked around. There was an entire aisle filled with best selling novels, those quick reads one takes on airplanes and then never knows whether it was the motion of the plane or the content of the novel that made one queasy in the gut. He spotted the latest Jerry Stevens book there, something about stolen nuclear warheads threatening Miami. It was described on the cover as "Explosive, hard-throbbing suspense with a generous dollop of horror tossed in, plus accurate, up to the minute technical descriptions of weaponry."

There were other store aisles devoted to children's soccer gear. There were two aisles of miniature electronic equipment, including cell phones that acted like computers, so that one could have the thrill of punching in messages on their miniature nine button sender holding all twenty six letters and in what amounted to finger torturing exercises. There were acres of hideous looking toys that made noise, mounds of candy bars, and, the special of the day, giant boxes of one-ply toilet paper.

While Jill shopped, showing a relentless will to save money, Mark rambled on about what was on his mind.

"I had dinner and a few drinks with a buddy of mine Wednesday night. He's a novelist, too. Marty McSorley?"

"Never heard of him. Did you talk about me?"

"We did in fact. And we talked about this publicity thing I am undergoing."

Jill, who seemed more interested in shopping than listening was following every word nonetheless.

"What about it?"

"Well Marty argued that I am simply childish when it comes to the Foss."

"Are you?"

"That is the idea confronting me at the moment."

"Where do I fit in, Slattery?"

Mark felt a flash of anger and spoke before he could stifle it.

"What do you want from me, Jill? A marriage proposal?"

She looked around at him, and went on shopping, trying to puff out a laugh but with her hurt showing instead. Mark, beginning to panic, hastened to apologize.

"Look, I am sorry. I don't mean to …"

"To marry me?"

Her smile returned in a flash, though her voice had a hard edge to it. Mark sighed. They were having their first confrontation and perhaps their last and only one. He decided to stick up for himself.

"No, I … wait. You never answer my calls. You only show up when you want. What do you want from me?"

"What do I want? What do you think, Slattery? Do you think I want to marry a man twenty-seven years my senior? You think I am one of those girls?"

"I don't know. Are you?"

"You are a good read, Slattery. But I can't very well give myself to a fictional hero."

"I am not Slattery."

"Yes you are, you dope."

"You think I'm childish?"

"You are not childish, Slattery, you are more what I would describe as insular. Tell me something. What would you do if you struck it rich, won the lottery or something? Would you give up your medical practice and just write novels?"

As they spoke they clogged an aisle so that irritated shoppers had to force their way past while grumbling.

"I've thought about that. No. I would do both. As it is I live in Manhattan, pay my bills, and have enough discretionary cash to take trips or vacations or … no. My life is nicely balanced."

"'Balanced?' Have you no needs?"

"Of course I do."

"Then why don't you marry again?"

"I was married."

"So?"

This last word was spit out with great force and this time with no attempt to disguise the anger behind it. Jill began walking again, taking greats strides and leaving Mark far behind. The two carts were so full by now he had difficulty pushing and dragging them. He had to call out from an aisle away.

"Help me out, will you?"

Jill was out of sight for nearly a minute. Finally she did appear and, without looking at him, took the lead cart and they made their way to a checkout line. They were silent during their wait until Jill insisted, "I believe I asked you a question."

"What question."

"I said … 'so?'"

"Oh, you mean about my divorce and … all that. Tell you what, Jill. After we unload this garbage in your tiny apartment you better come to mine and …"

"Yes?"

"And let me call the shots and let me have my way with you."

"Anything else?"

"Yes. I want you to know that I am not feeling so alone this moment."

She glared at him, and then softened.

"There is hope for you, Slattery."

Jill came to him that day. She came to him twice more the following week, but only after Mark did some serious begging.

It was six a. m. on a Thursday morning. Mark was seated at his desk in his apartment working on an outline for his next novel. His work went smoothly. He had already settled questions of narrative person and tense. He had his lead characters fleshed out, he had the setting and the mood down in notebook form, and he was well on his way to transforming his story into a workable plot. It struck him, as he sped along, how pleased he was with his work, his work ethic, his steady progress, and the fact that his devotion to his craft over all these years was at least paying these positive benefits.

It was not always like this.

In the beginning, staring from the day he finished college, it had been as frightening as having to walk into a wall of flames. In fact the anxiety associated with sitting down at a typewriter with a virgin piece of paper stuck in it was enough to cause those burning walls to close in on him, for writing novels meant growing up. Growing up, he realized, was different than simply being sensitive.

Eventually he was able to keep his rear end glued to the seat of his chair for four hours a night after working eight hours a day at some indifferent job. Four hours a night, with the anxiety conquered, meant he was disciplined enough to sit there and nothing else. Not one word was written on the blank page. Four hours a night for a year, just sitting there, grimly holding on while fighting with his childhood; that was all he had achieved.

"I will write."

"No, you will not."

Then came four hours a night for two more years, and all of it spent sitting on his rear end with nothing happening and nothing *to do* save that he allowed himself to look in the dictionary to keep from going mad. One day some real words started to come, happened to leak out, and of course the hair rose on the back of his neck, but even that cliché played itself out in just over a minute and he was back sitting there until he finally forced millions of words to come.

He worked his way into it by sheer willpower. After that came a year of experimental writing, tossing five hundred page scripts into the waste basket, and his practicing such common exercises as writing a book in the first person and then rewriting it in the third person and, throughout, Mark was learning his craft. It was then he woke up about the means of support, went to medical school but kept writing. He opened a practice and kept on writing. Finally he landed with Salter and Salter and here he was, separating the inner, where all these brave and virtuous deeds were being done, from the outer, where people like publishers and publicity agents threw it up into his face that he was not selling enough books.

It was only lately that he was coming to understand and appreciate that he had succeeded in launching himself into the alone and that the alone was not only aesthetical but ontological too. He was a creative writer. He was doing what he set out to do. He was content. Yet he was living this other messy life and still had no idea what he was to do about that.

At the insistence of the Foss, Mark promised to attend an agent conference for one weekend out in Easthampton, something he swore he would never do but now agreed to do anyway. It was the middle of April and the weather was cooperating; Jill was back playing hard to get and his practice was overwhelming him with paperwork. As he was packing to go Carrie Singleterry surprised him by dropping over to his apartment unannounced. When she heard his plans she said she would go with him, something that would have ordinarily delighted him but, in this case, left him feeling confused and vaguely uneasy. All he managed to say to her, and belatedly so, for Carrie had already been in his apartment for some minutes, was, “Where have you been, darling? I literally haven’t seen you in … what is it … how many weeks?”

She gave him a stern look, one that he had never seen her use before.

Mark?”

He could not believe it. She was using that tone of voice all women use when they wanted to slow down a man and make him feel positively dreadful. It worked. Mark stood there with head slightly bowed, suffering every icy word she hurled at him.

"We have an agreement, do we not? I let you work and you let me work. We see one another when we see one another. Has anything changed in this regard that I ought to know about?"

"No, no. You are right. I just … I missed you is all."

"Get over it. We all have our little feelings to deal with. But you are a big boy, Mark. Besides."

"Besides, what?"

"Things are happening on my job."

"Like what?"

"Well … even though the actual dates are up in the air … the word is I am up for chief buyer."

"Congratulations."

"Don't congratulate me just yet. This is a testing period. They want to see how committed I am. Which means there are times I need to be on the go day and night. It is my career, Mark."

"I am not holding you back, Carrie. I am just… glad to see you."

He gave her the details of the agent conference as they drove out to eastern Long Island in his car. Carrie, long used to networking, working the principle players at conferences, running meetings, and gaining victories during face to face business dealings, understood everything he said at once and long before they got to their destination it was clear to Mark that she knew even more about this conference and what was expected of him than he did. The actual location of the conference was a semi-private resort with some rooms overlooking the open water of the Atlantic. Arriving at reception, Carrie strode forward, every bit in charge, while Mark hung back, not at all in charge.

"This is going to be great," Carrie boomed out while Mark struggled with luggage. "Go look at the dinner menu, darling. I'll handle check in."

Thinking back on that weekend some days later, Mark did not know whether to curse aloud, or merely laugh bitterly.

This is what happened.

Once they checked in they discovered that although there were a dozen agents promised, about one for every ten hopeful writers who had not only paid six hundred a night to be there in Easthampton but had forked out a one thousand dollar entrance fee as well, that only four of these agents were actually in attendance. Three of them were strictly non-fiction specialists and the one fiction agent, a man named Roy Roberts, of the vaunted Roy Roberts Agency, informed all hopefuls, including Mark, and this within an hour of his checking in, "I am taking on no new clients at this time."

Mark, ignoring all the advice Carrie was giving him about his demeanor, snapped back at once.

"If you are not taking any more clients then what the hell are you doing here? For that matter, what am I doing here?"

Roy, a tall, emaciated, balding, arrogant, New York personage, whose arms floated free of his body like the wings of some wading bird, looked at Mark as if deciding to dismiss him from this earth merely by evoking some sort of class distinction and answered, with a generous unleashing of his Park Avenue coolness,

"Perhaps you need a lesson in … place. Though I cannot see it doing you any good at your advanced age. Try to get it into your head that I have clients who patiently waited for my nod through ten or more of these conferences before I finally turned to them … in an act of kindness. They showed patience first, and appreciation later. This being so, this being the case, I can only wonder what it is that gives you the idea that you ought to be considered out of turn. You, Mark Forrest, are nothing more than some dismissible little scribbler from Salter and Salter, one of the shakier publishing houses in all of New York."

Mark was ready to go home at once but Carrie, who was by now enjoying herself immensely, and who had managed to greet and meet one of the three non-fiction agents, a Miss Samuels, of the Rice and Bowles Agency, was determined to stay. She gave Mark her patient smile and spoke to him softly but firmly.

"I know this is not your thing, darling, and I know that Roy is not willing to talk to you, but it will not hurt you to mingle with the other authors and get some networking in. Do it for me, darling? Besides, I need to talk with Sherry about something. OK?"

"Who the hell is Sherry?"

"That is Miss Samuels."

Mark agreed to stay though he spent the two days glaring at the other authors and refusing to talk to them, walking alone on the wind-whipped beach, getting more than a bit drunk on beer, and standing like a fool, in the shadows at the back of the dining room, spying on Carrie and Sherry as they sat with their heads together with their tongues constantly wagging.

From a distance of twenty yards Carrie looked more rounded to him than Mark remembered. Her honey blonde hair and her olive skin ran together like blended interior wall paints so that she appeared, about the neck, like the hunter's moon in a hazy sky just before dawn.

"She looks forty, at least," Mark breathed out from his hiding place behind a fake palm tree.

Used to seeing Carrie in sweaters, Mark was further disconcerted to observe her in her best work clothes. Her tailored suits, which appeared to have come off the same rack at Ann Taylor's as did Sherry Samuel's, made her look not so much rounded as it did plain fat.

"Jesus."

Carrie and Mark had breakfast together on Saturday but after that he was left completely on his own as Carrie and Sherry took their subsequent meals together. When Mark strode across the dining room seeking to intervene he was sent away with cold stares. He and Carrie did not speak to one another in their room that Saturday night, though Carrie displayed no signs of irritation and seemed oblivious to his presence, his mood, and his person. The conference ended Sunday afternoon and on their way back to Manhattan Carrie ended a long, strained silence by launching into the following monologue.

"I learned a lot this weekend, Mark. I learned that this is the only way to do business in the book business. In fact, this is the only way to do any sort of business. This is how it is done. It is basic. It is elementary. Your world is no different from my world. To recognize this is to recognize the difficulty facing publishers and agents in a shrinking market; it is what every author is expected to grasp. You have to come to them! You should not bristle at that and think you are merely kissing their ass. That is the market; that is the reality of it. I just cannot fathom why you haven't gone to these conferences before. I know you are a good writer and that you are sensitive and that you are a loner and that you are serious and that you are proud and that you are standing behind your novels and … all of that. Furthermore, you know that I am sympathetic to you and have been in your corner all this time and have been willing to coddle you within limits and … all of that. Think of it this way: your refusing to cooperate at these conferences would be like my refusing to go to Asia now that the clothes are being made there because of some sensitive hang up I might have about Asians. I have to do my job no matter what! You need to do yours. Writing is not your entire job. Salter and Salter put you on notice and you are still having trouble filtering that message through your noggin. Mark, I know you are fifty-two and I know it is hard to get in step with what is happening in this changing world but it is ultimately your responsibility to be responsible. You can't expect me to bail you out on this. These agents have no reason to take a new client on in a shrinking market. They have to make money on the client list they already have and that is what you have to crack into. Now don't give me that look! You know what that look reminds me of? One of those Dostoievsky character looks. Right! You know perfectly well what I am going to say, like when someone is trying to tell the hero what is good for him and trying to have an adult exchange with him and the hero, rather than taking responsibility for his half of this adult conversation, decides to record what the other person is saying so that they can enter it into their journal or diary as a juicy bit of writing to titillate their readers. That is exactly it, isn't it? Don't try to deny it. I know that look on your face. You think you can make juicy fiction out of this. I *know* you are thinking that way. Meantime you are evading your responsibilities. So what if Roy blew you off the first time? You have to keep at him, you have to learn to be smooth, you have to network, Mark. Roy was just testing you to see if you have the toughness to come back at him. Now Sherry and I … oh … I might as well come straight out and tell you the facts. Sherry liked my suit, the one I wore Friday night … you never commented on it … and we got talking about my job as a buyer and I happened to tell her that I travel the world looking for items to select and buy and she started asking me some really penetrating questions about what is involved in buying clothes for a top New York apartment store in this changing and exciting global market economy and how women are traveling the world by themselves … that being a side bar issue … and before I knew it you know what? Sherry said she was taking me on as a client and we are going to meet at her offices this very week to discuss a book deal she says she can put together with a publisher. How about that? That is the way you do it, Mark. That is the book business."

Chapter Seven

There was a call from the Foss. Mark, thinking that it was about his performance amongst the dentists, soon realized it was not. Instead he was summoned to an unscheduled meeting so she could "update" him on their limited business arrangement. Noting a defensive tone in her voice, Mark's insides hardened. By now the novelist was growing as tough as nails when it came to this book selling business, even if he was learning nothing practical about selling books. His experience with publicity came to treating it with cynicism, something both Carrie and Jill could only shake their heads over and go on to wonder if there was any hope for him at all. He waited until Foss's voice trailed off and shot back, "I will agree to meet with you if and only if it is not at your office."

"Not at … what is wrong with meeting me there?"

"I cannot take the color scheme, Ms. Foss, and I won't."

She demurred, named a restaurant-bar on Madison Avenue and he went straight there after closing up his office on Tuesday. They shook hands, stiffly, then sat in the window and ordered martinis. Mark was wearing a new suit; Ms. Foss was poured into a pink dress with what he took to be flounces. Her hair dye was toned down this time out; no longer the color of egg yokes, Mark judged it to be more like diluted cadmium yellow. Her face powder was every bit as dense, however, and he had to refrain from asking her if she had encountered any enemy fire on the way to their meeting.

"Cheers," she offered, holding out her drink glass so he could touch it with his.

"Cheers," he echoed.

The Foss was not only on the defensive; she was doing her best to be friendly. Mark still couldn't see his way clear to taking advantage of the fact that he was, for the moment anyway, the stronger one. It was obvious that whenever she delivered opportunities he fumbled them away, and whenever she withdrew opportunities the adult in him froze while the child in him leered. They drank quickly, exchanging pleasantries and, after ordering a second round of drinks Ms. Foss got down to business. Her voice was conciliatory.

"I know it says on your list that I have booked you onto the top television book-review show."

She faltered after this and Mark took up the slack.

"Yes. I know. I am looking forward to that. It's the only show where I can talk intelligently about *Bleak,* and with an intelligent host, and without interruption."

"That is true but now we have a hitch."

"Oh?"

"Two hitches, really."

"Go on, I am listening."

"First of all the show is shamefully overbooked. Too many authors and their agents and their publicists have been promised time and the hard reality is there isn't enough time for everyone. I was taken in like everyone else in my business. I am like a travel agent who operates on good faith only to be duped by the airline industry."

Mark, who only knew enough to be cynical, tried to press.

"All that may be so, but *somebody* is getting on every week. What distinguishes those who are still getting on the show from those who are suddenly deemed 'overbooked'? No! Don't tell me. I will tell you. Those who pay more, those who pay over and above what they are already paying are the one's getting on. Am I right?"

Ms. Foss shook her head slowly.

"You haven't learned much, Dr. Forrest. No. There is no gouging going on."

"What then?"

"Never mind, we … I might as well get to the second reason. The show is going out of business."

This stunned Mark.

"What? Ever since I was a kid this was *the* show for authors. We all watched it. We still do. I don't catch it every time out but it is the most popular show we know of. I … we … rely on it."

"On the contrary, the ratings are dismal. The popular audience is not there."

"But I thought…"

"Mark! Wake up. In 1967 that show was on in prime time. Now the tapes are played after midnight. That is why you are not watching every time out. You are asleep! And from our end, from the publicity end, who gives a tinker's damn how many starving novelists are watching the show? They don't add up to enough people; they do not buy products; they do not generate revenue. The people who do buy things, the people who might be induced to buy your book, watch only main stream television."

"You mean A. C. Cottonwood."

"Are you still upset with him? He is small time compared to some of the afternoon shows. I am talking about … Mark? Dr. Forrest? Read the small print. I am not going to give you any of your money back but I can do something for you in return. To fulfill this little gap in the contract."

"What?"

"I can get you on the Beagle Show."

Mark stared at her in disbelief. The Beagle Show was a spin-off of the Jerry Springer show, a time slot where low life couples talked about their body odors or about what they took to be their more interesting bowl movements, where they struck one another below the belt and where heavyset guests tried to tear off all their clothes before being stopped by security guards. Ms. Foss rushed on.

"Forty-two million viewers tune into this show every day. Granted, some of them haven't bought a single book in their entire lives but listen to this; Grover Glide, the producer, called my mother with an idea. He wants a real writer to appear on the Beagle Show and 'educate' the viewers on the literary scene. I know, I know, the other guests will be competing with you and they can be … they are encouraged to be outrageous but still … if you agree to do this you will have sales. Beagle Show viewers do what they are told."

"It has come to this?"

Of a sudden Ms. Foss tossed down most of her second martini and her tough stance returned before the alcohol lit up the inside of her generous belly.

"You are not selling, Doctor. You are not responding to my help. If I am going to help you we have to do something radical. You are the one came to my mother's agency in the first place, may I remind you. You are the one who wrote the check. Do you want to do this or not?"

"I will not get down with the vulgar."

"You will have to. Novel writing is no different than politics save that it doesn't pay nearly as well."

"I cannot do this."

"Why not?"

"Because bad language drives out good language."

"What is that supposed to mean?"

"That I cannot do it, I will not do it. No."

For a moment Ms. Foss's hard glance lingered, but then, in yet another unexpected reversal, it softened again. She even went so far as to place her generous hand over his undersized one. She said to him, as if revealing the secret of the century,

"You are not a hack."

"Are you complimenting me?"

The hand patted and massaged. The glance grew misty. The tone of voice was dulcet.

"What I am saying is this. You are like Dostoievsky's Idiot. You are too innocent to be walking around in this city. Look, I ... I will book you into some alternate sites. Some lesser venues where you can make your own pitch, read from your book, whatever. Do your best."

After that she sat there like a luridly painted, middle-aged actress playing the ingénue, and Mark had a horrible awareness strike him; the women was waiting for him to invite her to have dinner.

"Waiter!"

He paid for the drinks and was away within five minutes, leaving her sitting in the window looking like one of those women on display on a certain street in Amsterdam.

Slattery's bleak adventure in the novel, *Bleak,* was supposed to be unusual. As a hero he did not slay dragons, or win the girl, or lead the troops in or out of Moscow. What he did instead was voyage in and out of a bleak aesthetic landscape, pitting that against the merely pretty. His adversaries included the sentimental, and the conventional. Slattery's evolving vision of the world unfolded in a series of vignettes in which the phenomenal world became continuously bleaker and thus more aesthetically pleasing.

This delicate balancing act required a good deal of skill on Mark's part, or so he judged: he let Slattery envision essences instead of facts, forms instead of particulars, and characteristic definitions instead of shapes. The bleak, his entry point, became the portal to Beauty itself. Slattery's adventure was not for those who tuned into the Beagle Show, nor was it for the likes of A. C. Cottonwood and his band of media monsters. It was a journey through a world of pure art.

In the novel Slattery continued living in the mundane world. His wife still saw to it that he took out the garbage, the light company made sure he paid his bill on time, and the prunes returned to their husbands and recalled, on many a long winter's evening, and with automatic shudders, that awful, silent, staring man who had ruined their shopping trip in Phoenix by making them feel so terribly self-conscious. As Jill put it to the author of *Bleak,* "There wasn't a hell of a lot of plot in your last novel, Slattery. Just thought it best if I mention that to the author."

On the first day of May Carrie instructed Mark to meet her at one of their favorite haunts, a tiny restaurant on the upper public floor at Trump Tower.

"Seven is OK? You make sure you get there on time. I might be late. If I am, go ahead and order a decent bottle of wine."

Mark did as he was told. He and Carrie had little to say to one another since their trip to Easthampton. She was not sleeping at his place, and though they did meet for dinner now and again their conversations were marathons of breezy, rapid-fire clichés delivered through strained lips. Mark asked no questions about her work and Carrie provided no news. The new lack of candor in their relationship exhausted both of them, and Mark assumed this evening would provide more of the same. He was wrong.

He was all the way through the first bottle of wine he ordered and was sipping the first glass of the second when Carrie showed up very late and in a whirl, her eyes glowing and her olive skin glistening. She was decidedly heavier than she was a month previously. Mark had all he could do to stop himself from comparing her growing bulk to the more established flesh of the Foss.

He stood up to kiss her. She turned her lips away at the last moment and he bussed her cheek instead. The odor of expensive perfume tickled his nostrils. He noted that her hair was newly dyed. It was no longer honey blonde; it was more like egg yoke. Sitting down with a flourish and taking Mark in with one decisive glance, she said, "You are drunk, doctor."

"Well I haven't eaten all day. I was up early writing and had a busy time at the office and…"

"That is not criticism, darling. Just staring a fact."

Carrie had abandoned her sweater look and Mark had not gotten used to her more formal, business attire, though she never did seek his opinion on her clothes. They went through a few moments of embarrassed silence. Mark used the bowing waiter as an excuse to ignore this, ordering food and thus not suffering eye contact with his long standing, New York girlfriend. This diversion did not last and it was not until they were spooning their leek soup that Carrie took over.

"Mark? I got the head buyer job."

"Oh good. That is great news, darling. When do you start?"

He had considered standing up and kissing her again but somehow thought better of it.

"Officially, not till August, but they have me bombarded with tasks already and … I guess they are letting me get used to the increased load."

"It is all going to unfold here in Manhattan though, right?"

Carrie pursed her lips and rolled her eyes. Mark thought, *"Jill Cartwright can eat no fat, Carrie cat eat no lean."*

"That *is* true as far as corporate headquarters goes. The department store is located here and so are its executive offices. But the buyer's business spans many locations. New York, Dallas, even Tokyo."

"You'll be doing a lot more traveling, then?"

"Not so much … traveling … as … ah … being in different locations. If you follow me."

"Not really."

"I am being promoted to company jet status. My job makes me global. I am going to be working and living in the world."

"What can I say? Congratulations."

Carrie looked at Mark to see if he was making fun of her but he was smiling so hard his cheek muscles hurt. Her searching look lingered for some seconds. Before she continued she looked down at her hands and played with her napkin. When she raised her face to meet his again, she was holding her breath.

"Yes?" he asked. "What else?"

She hesitated, then said, matter-of-factly, "Mark, I got the book deal I told you about, the one with Sherry?"

"Did you."

"Yes. There is a book deal and … we think … a media deal as well."

"What do you mean a 'media deal'?"

"You know."

"No, I don't."

"Sherry is setting it up so one of the television networks does a documentary special on me. About a woman breaking down business barriers in the big city and all that."

"I thought buyers were mostly woman anyway."

"They are, that is true, but in my case …"

"Yes?"

"Oh, Mark, you don't understand a thing. Sherry can make me hot."

"Really?"

"We've got New York, we've got the global angle, we've got jet setting, we've got fashion, and … we've got it all."

"Who is going to write the book? You?"

For the first time Carrie's anger showed. It was not pretty. She managed to control herself, barely, by downing the wine in her glass and then tapping the glass so that Mark could refill it. When she spoke again it was through stiffened lips.

"The TV special, if we pull it off, will be made in conjunction with the book's publication. Who the hell writes the copy is of no account. Sherry says she has lackeys can do that sort of job in a week. What counts is promotion."

"Are you going to use the Caraway firm for that?"

"We might."

At this, Mark lost his nerve and just sat there. Carrie waited a few seconds before handing him more.

"Mark, I am pulling out of our relationship."

His mouth moved. His consciousness heard. Though he was already far, far away. He spoke feebly.

"You don't have to do that, Carrie. I know you are busy but … you are already so busy that I hardly ever see you."

"Are you saying you like it this way?"

"What's to complain about?" he lied. He thought, *"I am lying to her because I am afraid to tell her I have fallen in love with a younger woman who doesn't even bother to return my phone calls."*

"Mark?"

"Yes?"

"We could not go on as we were. You must admit as much."

"I admit to nothing of the sort."

Carrie sighed so loud it sounded like dragon's breath. She bared her small, even teeth and there was no question about it; she was deeply enraged.

"Mark, if you were a gentleman you would allow me to leave graciously. You would respect my private interests and let me go. Don't you see? I have been spending all this time asking you to let me go."

"And I have been assuring you that you have all the independence you need. That is the essence of our relationship. Is it not?"

"Goddamn you, Mark. Do you want me to say it? You asked for it. I not only have a promotion and a book deal, I have someone else in my life. Do you get it? Do you finally get something? I have another man. I am sleeping with him and I am not going to sleep with him and you, too. There."

"Who?"

"What the hell do you want to know that for? Are you some sort of masochist?"

"No, I … no. I am just curious is all; I mean you have been so busy for so long and …"

"There you go. Suspecting me. You think that just because I have been working hard this last year that I had to have another man."

"No, I … well."

"Well I did not have a man."

"But you just said …"

"I just met this man a month ago if you must know."

"Well if you have this new job and are going global and are busy around the clock then how can you see this guy more than you see me?"

She looked at him and sighed anew.

"Mark … you really do not get it. We … busy people … find time for one another."

"So … he is a busy boy, too. Did you meet him on a jet?"

"You really want to know?"

"Yes. Not to torture myself, but just to know."

"I work with Sherry late at night when I get off work. I am drawn into two worlds, the world of the buyer and the world of literary agents. And I … it was a natural … I started dating Roy."

"Roy fucking Roberts!"

Everyone in the restaurant turned around to stare. Carrie's face took on a severely disproving look as well and, after a few moments of silence, a silence designed to allow Mark to regain what little social grace he had left, she went on, speaking to him the way a mother explains death to a little child.

"I just could not forgive you for the way you treated Roy at that conference, Mark. I just could not."

"How I treated him? As I remember it, he was the one to put me down. He called me … and my publishing house … a … never mind."

Carrie was through sighing. She was at the point where she saw it was no use trying to continue. She was like a cat owner who finally admits that the pet cannot listen to reason.

"You don't get it, Mark. Roy is a great man."

"He's an *agent.* He represents novelists. He is a wormy businessman. It is the writer who…"

"Mark? Hasn't Ms. Foss taught you anything? Writers, including fiction writers, are tools to be plugged in during the business process."

"So, Roy is a big man and I am a lackey, an outdated tool he cares not to use."

"Put it any way you want."

"Carrie … one more thing."

"Yes?"

"Ah … if I was to make up a fictional account of all this …"

"Yes?"

"Would this be the moment of pathos? Would this be the unexpected plot twist? Or would this be the inevitable outcome of dealing with my personal character? I mean I really want to know."

"I don't know what you are talking about. You are lost in your own interior."

She made ready to get up and leave him alone at the table but he grasped her wrist and held her in her chair.

"One more thing."

"What!"

"What is it like screwing Roy Roberts? I mean does it make you throw up? Is that what you have to do, vomit your way to the top of the business world?"

She tore her hand away and was gone, nearly tipping over the table as she went. Mark sat there seething. He knew where he was right about Carrie and where he was wrong about Carrie, and yet he did not give a damn about the latter position; he was upset with her for leaving him before he had secured Jill and he was jealous of her success in the literary world and beyond.

Chapter Eight

Mark left several telephone calls for Jill telling her he had broken it off with his long time girl friend. He did not trouble his conscience over the little added lie that *he* was the one who had ended the relationship. Jill did not respond. Mark, alarmed by day, uneasy at night, and with the growing suspicion that he had been double-crossed, dropped by her studio three times yet never managed to catch her at home, unless she was home and would not answer the buzzer.

"Now what?"

As this silence continued he vowed not to panic or to declare himself a fool. Nevertheless he grew the more anxious and with only this for compensation; Jill had established control of their affair from the outset. Still, he was in love with a woman much younger than himself, one who had more or less indicated, and on more than one occasion, that she would continue to play hard to get, but only so long as he was playing her off against his long time girlfriend. He had done his bit; the ball was now in Jill's court. She was, by continuing to play hard to get, not playing at all. Mark felt sorry for himself, which was nothing new to him: as well he wondered what Slattery would do.

Then, late on a Monday afternoon in June, when Mark and Janie were the only ones left in his office and were closing down for the day, Jill Cartwright breezed into the waiting room unannounced. Janie saw her first.

"I am sorry, Miss. We are just leaving. You can call answering service if you want to make an appointment."

The two women measured one another critically, that is to say with sweeping, cat-like, hair-to-shoes glances of disapproval.

"I don't need to make an appointment," Jill shot back, her tone of voice as jaunty as her bouncy, angular bodily movements. She looked terribly thin and young in a black tee shirt and torn blue jeans, but it was a look that accentuated the neo-bohemian image she carried along with her short cropped, glossy black hair, her large, brilliantly shining blue eyes, and her startling, elfin ears.

There was an outrageousness to her look as well, what with her taut cheekbones protruding out on either side of her inexplicably large, fleshy nose, so that the total presentation lent her a smoky, Nineteen-thirties, cabaret look, a defiant demeanor that could be taken even further should she decide to add lurid green eye shadow and purple-tinted rouge. She appeared, for that alone, an exotic woman, not in the way a foreign beauty is exotic because of her rareness, but because she seemed a throwback to eras highlighted by behavioral recklessness, hot jazz, and rumors of bold sensual excess, eras not commonly embraced by Twenty-first century New Yorkers. Janie, not prepared for such an onslaught, was taken aback.

"Are you a patient of Dr. Forrest?"

"No. I am his only remaining girl friend. I have come to claim him. That is, if my ticket is still good."

Mark entered the waiting room that moment and an awkward moment it was. He had only hours earlier broken the news to Janie about what had happened to him and Carrie, but without saying a word about Jill. Janie had of course assumed that she was finally going to take Carrie's place.

"You are his … Mark!"

"Ah … this is not … ah …"

Jill grasped everything unfolding before her in this one take. It helped that Mark had in passing mentioned this loyal employee, Janie, and her romantic misconceptions during one of their pillow talks, and she vowed to control and diffuse the situation at once. She took a firm stride toward the bushy-haired woman, held out her hand for shaking, and asked, in a take charge voice, "Your name is?"

"Janie."

"Janie, hi. I am Jill Cartwright. I am preparing for my doctoral defense in literature … this fall I hope … and Mark and I have discovered we have much in common, and all of that to do with his novels. Isn't that right, Slattery?"

Jill beamed a smile at Mark, who was still so flustered he could not get his voice to register an entire sentence.

"Ah …"

Janie, extracting her hand from Jill's, wheeled to Mark as well.

"Mark … this … person is … what to you?"

"Ah …"

Jill answered for him.

"Slattery is mine."

"Who is Slattery?" Janie shouted out in hot anger. Jill put her hand over her heart in mock surprise.

"Haven't you read his novel, *Bleak,* Janie?"

"His novel? I am only concerned with Dr. Forrest's medical practice."

"There you go. You think of Dr. Forrest as an internist first, last, and always. You think of his novel writing as a hobby he takes up in his free time, one that you might cure him of if given the chance. But medicine is at best his means of support. It has its own context and its own enclosure. You are his best gal, I take it; but I am his girl."

That was enough. It was not until Janie, hot tears of rage streaming down her cheeks, left the office slamming the door behind her, her hair bouncing over the collar of her coat like so much cotton candy caught in a slight breeze, that Jill turned her attention to Mark straight up.

"So! You give me no credit, Slattery."

"Huh?"

"You say it was *you* who broke it off with your old girlfriend? I have my doubts. Why, you obviously haven't even gone out of your way to explain to that poor woman, Janie, what her proper place is in the overall schema of your life."

"Jill! What are you doing here? Where have you been?"

"Deciding whether or not I really want to hook up with the old fart with a faint heart."

"Is that true?"

"Yes. It has been hard for me of late."

Mark finally woke up to the point where he was able to stride across the waiting room, take Jill in his arms, and kiss her. She let him do this but during the subsequent hug she went right on with the explication of her second thoughts, her voice reverberating in the fold of his left shoulder.

"I keep telling myself I don't want to settle for a man who cannot conjoin his aesthetic talent with his worldly aplomb or his lack thereof."

"Me?"

"Yes, you. This is you all over, Slattery. You are such a passive bungler. And I hate to think of myself as being the woman who takes you in tow … voluntarily. Women are always swearing not to do that but then doing just that … when it really makes more sense for them to hold out for a man who can take care of himself."

"I love you, Jill. Do you love me?"

"Oh, Slattery. Do you think that saying 'I love you' solves anything?"

"I love you. Do you love me?"

"Damn it all … yes."

"Well, then."

"Well then, nothing."

"But if we love one another …"

"If we love one another it means I get stuck with you and have to manage you. Listen. Lock this place up. I'm taking you to a bookstore."

They walked quickly, ending up at one of the large chain bookstores on Fifth Avenue. As they wandered the aisles Jill asked, "What do you think of a place like this?"

"I like it … at least the fiction section. I like the idea of gathering a bunch of novels together and I like seeing my own titles sitting alphabetically in the F's. Of course, there are none of my books on display today. I am not exactly on fire. I mean, there were a couple of copies of my novels here but they have sold."

"Are you complaining about that?"

"Sometimes I think it is better to have a book on display unsold than it is to have it sold with no more coming."

"That's it? That is your take on this bookstore?"

"What more do you want? That is how serious writer's think."

Jill took Mark's hand and led him back towards the front of the store the way a mother leads her son towards a public rest room. On the way she asked, "Who did the blurbs for your novels, Slattery?"

"Oh, those. Ryan asked some famous novelists and they all turned him down. So I got blurbs from some less than famous writers who … writers with whom I identify."

"Which did not help your sales, right?"

"I guess not."

"Ryan doesn't work very hard for you."

"Well, over at Salter and Salter they … I don't know. I did have a three-book contract. I am going to meet with him next week about the future. I am going to present my latest outlines."

"Doesn't it strike you as ominous that they pulled promotion on *Bleak*"

"Well, I …"

"Yours was not a publication, Slattery. It was a Privacation."

"Huh?"

"They are letting you sink into oblivion while covering themselves legally and financially. They made a decision about you."

"What decision is that?"

"That you are not now nor ever will be a best seller."

"But that is … true. It was always true."

"You think they always thought that?"

"Why … yes!"

"Slattery. You are a child. Here. Look at this table. What does it say?"

"New Arrivals."

"Tell me something. When your three books came out, did they get onto this table? I mean before they were slotted on the alphabetical shelves in the fiction section."

"Ah … come to think of it … no."

"What does that tell you?"

"What is it supposed to tell me?"

"Slattery, that is an integral part of promotion. Someone has to pay money, up front, to get a book stationed on this shelf at the front of the store where customers, coming in off the street, will brose first. This is a shelf that sells books. You never thought of that?"

"I guess … no."

"Do you really love me, Slattery?"

"I do."

"Have you ever asked me what I am going to do once I get my doctorate? Are you even a bit curious?"

"No, I … I just assume you would look for a university teaching job."

"I hope to teach on the side. I want to keep a foot in academe but what I really want to do is become a literary agent. That is good news for you down the line, Slattery. You understand that much."

"I do."

"How do you understand it?"

"Huh?"

"Let me explain something to you. There is a natural crossover between literary critics in academe and literary professionals working in publishing, and in promotion, and in agencies. It is no different than the flitting back and forth people do between the Pentagon and commercial defense contractors. People have a choice; they can merely concentrate on sales, looking at the short run each time out, or they can be far-forward looking and seek to enhance a single writer's reputation for the long haul."

"You mean you … would do that for me?"

"Jesus! Slattery? Why else would I…"

"Oh. Ah …"

"What?"

"Can we go to my place now?"

Lying in bed some hours later, and with Jill nestled in his arms and breathing softly, Mark, unable to sleep, separated out several disparate considerations concerning him and his new girl friend, and in relation to the other women that had slept beside him.

Yes he was in love again at age fifty-two. He thought about Jill day and night, he was overwhelmed with desire for her, he was drowning in emotion, he was ruled by passion, he was completely circumscribed by her presence, and he was rushing along in the flood of deep, hot, soul-expanding consciousness that her reciprocating love offered him. Yet he was reflective enough to remember having been in love twice before in his life. He had fallen in love with the woman he had married, Mattie, and what did that amount to? His love for Mattie had to compete with his insistence on very long working days, four hours of which was spent writing novels, the rest for practicing medicine. Then there was Mattie's disillusionment with the big city and her lack of personal development. When they broke up, and when Mattie went back to Idaho, wasn't a residue of love still there between them, and didn't it hurt like hell, and didn't he survive the hurt regardless?

Mark sighed, thinking that love is an ocean, Idaho is a state, and Manhattan is a state of mind. A man and a woman can drown in the ocean of love all they want, but they still have to conduct their separate lives while time moves on.

He had loved Carrie while they were together and he had *fallen* in love with Carrie when they first met. Now he was consumed with love for Jill. He was drowning for the third time but was, as well, twice jaded. Ultimately love was the same for him; it was the women he loved who were different.

As for sex, what he enjoyed with Jill was the honeymoon phase for sure. Yet he had enjoyed a honeymoon with Mattie and another one with Carrie, the only qualitative differences being that with each added honeymoon he was growing older while his women were growing younger. These facts were not to be ignored, along with the further one that all honeymoons came to an end and who could predict that, ten years from now, he would be able to declare that sex with Jill was positively better than sex with Carrie, or Mattie? Such was the fate of one who changes life partners.

Then there was the reality of rotating bodies. Mark's body, at fifty-two was one thing; Mattie's body was another thing, Carrie body another thing again, and Jill's body was once again another thing again. Objectively speaking, Mattie had had a terrific body while she was young, she had been better looking that Carrie or Jill could ever hope to be, though the last time he saw his ex-wife she was looking square and dense, as if she had been taking in corn syrup solids for added bulk. Meantime Carrie's body, once considered pear-like had now rounded off and to the point where he was tempted to call her the amorphous one. Yet Jill's body was so terribly thin, he already could anticipate a day arriving when he would prefer looking at her in designer clothes rather than staring at her walking naked out of the shower.

Plus, no matter how young a woman was when he got involved with her, she aged regardless. Still, none of these aging women were going to catch up to him. Mattie and Carrie, too, had managed to escape having to take care of him as his aging body marched him towards decrepitude. Surely Jill must have weighed that into consideration during this recent period when she refused to answer his calls. Yet all this physical stuff told him that he was a physician after all. He knew bodies. Bodies fail us. Bodies fall apart.

"It is not about bodies," he whispered into the dark.

What was it about, then?

Even though he had his talent and his medical practice, Mark had to admit that all human beings are weak and finite and in constant need to help.

"We all need somebody. What does that come to?"

There was this difference between his marriage to Mattie and his relationships with Carrie and Jill. The last two women were sympathetic to his work. And he was sympathetic to their work, to their becoming New York women, to the development of their potentialities. He had given Carrie his full blessing and then what? She had left him anyway. Having a loving person who is both sympathetic to your work and is being reciprocal, too, is no guarantee that things will last.

"No kidding," he whispered.

Mark glanced at the luminous dial of the clock on the bedside table. It was ten minutes to four. He had thoroughly played out this love and life business; if he was not going to get to sleep tonight he might as well return to the basics.

"I am a novelist. At bottom I am ruled by my aesthetic drive and not my knowledge of bodies and their fate."

Mark remembered, as if it was a second ago, as if memory and consciousness were not as yet two phenomena but still one explosive presence, the moment he learned to read. He was plunged into a world of magic from which he had never, ever returned unscathed.

"Is that the same as or different from love?"

"It is different. It is the same."

The adult writer chases the magic world experienced by the child, transforms it into sets of words, thus bringing the reader into the magic circle and thus expanding the joy of literature. That is what counts.

"That is what the Foss denies. She denies the magic."

The magic?

Mark remembered, with irritation, walking by a grammar school in the west fifties one Wednesday afternoon when the youngsters were pouring out onto the street after being released from their classes. Knots of children had already gathered and, as he passed them, his steps slowed because of the crowding, he overheard them talking about "magic." What was magical to them was not their hot plunge into literature-as-love but the fact that they all watched and adored some television show then current and swearing that it was *that* show that made their lives deep and worthwhile. Mark had seen this particular television show and knew it to be altogether trite, filled with braying nonsense, bad acting, the lowest order of shrill histrionics, and that it was devoid of any meaningful content.

"What does that mean?" he thought.

It meant victory for the Foss's of this world in the sense that negotiations between one's inner life and one's outer life are best controlled by strong, smart, business-savvy people who occupy offices in big cities, and who know the value of a dollar.

Sighing, trembling, confused, Mark buried his face in Jill's taut cheek and waited for his tears to spill out onto her flesh.

Novelist Mark Forrest entered the lobby of a blunt, bland, eighteen story building on lower Park Avenue, negotiated his steps around some workman doing business at the directory, and pushed the elevator button for the fourth floor, where were located the offices of Salter and Salter Publishing. He had not been here since the publication of *Bleak* but had with him several novel outlines, some sample chapters of each, as well as two entire manuscripts of earlier work he thought might be of interest to Ryan. He had to smile as he went up in the lift speaking to himself.

"Good old Ryan. I was always able to convince him of what was good for S. and S. It is a comfort."

Mark's idealistic rendering of his past encounters with Ryan Salter continued to titillate him as he gained the fourth floor and made his way to the big glass door at the far end of the hallway. He pictured kindly Ryan Salter as having a light coating of literary dust on his business suit. The man was a Columbia grad who was ever solicitous to the needs and wants and moods of the authors he dealt with; he was the opposite of all the Ms. Fosses of the world. When dealing with Ryan, Mark, felt that he was secretly in charge of whatever negotiations transpired, though not to the point of making it explicit.

"Come in."

Mark's grin faded a bit when he entered the office in real time. The furniture was more expensive looking than he remembered, the desk was larger, and Ryan himself looked anything but pliable and sympathetic. There was no dust on his suit. It was a Hickey Freeman number that made the young publisher appear very sharp.

"Sit down, Mark."

"Yes, I … hello."

Mark sat down in a chair with tight wooden sides and at once began fumbling with his bag of scripts and outlines, his hands trembling a little. Ryan just stared at him over the large desk.

"I've brought … here. I have the outlines and … but I don't know if you remember … I have entire scripts here that you can look at. There is that one about the woman who thinks she is thinking in another body other than her own … do you … the woman who has a kind of Virginia Woolf awareness? And I have the one about the guy who goes of the Museum of Modern Art every day to …ah … you know."

Ryan said nothing. Then he looked at his watch. Mark, catching this gesture, changed course.

"Oh but perhaps I better just turn over the outlines of the new stuff."

Ryan drank coffee from a large mug and made a depreciative, smacking noise with his lips. After hesitating for a split second he began to speak.

"This is an awkward time of the year, Mark. We couldn't possibly look at your work now."

"Why not?"

"Well ... you know how it is ... June? Everyone is getting ready to go out to the Hamptons. And you know how little work gets done there."

Mark, not only confused, but rendered childlike as well, tried to play off this.

"Yes, you are right ... the Hamptons. I could leave these anyway and then in September, when everyone is back they could ..."

"September is bad. That is when we will be up to our elbows putting together the Christmas list."

"The Christmas list ... yes. That is a busy time. When, then ... when do you think you will get to me?"

Ryan, looking more and more corporate and less and less like the young man who used to quote passages from Christopher Isherwood's first novel, *All the Conspirators,* to a group of young novelists at a bar on upper Broadway and as an example of the pure aesthetic dominating, looked at his watch a second time and said, in a voice totally devoid of any sympathy, "Mark, we no longer feel you are helping us here at Salter and Salter."

Mark heard what was said to him, added to that what he had been advised by the Foss and by Jill, and did his best to reject the whole of it.

"Ryan ... what are ... I am your ... all the novelists you publish are just like me."

Ryan spoke back like a businessman.

"That was never really the case. We have always had an interest in making money. It was just that the reading public was used to a bit of finery back when. But that was back then."

"Yes but Salter and Salter doesn't change its values."

The man stared at Mark with growing disgust.

"I guess you are the last one to get it. The news is that Salter and Salter is turning to popular culture. We have induced Jerry Stevens to join us, along with several good writers who can pump out books that people on the go are willing to read."

It was too much to bear.

"Ryan? I count you as a fan of my writing. You are a fan of serious writing and …"

"What the hell is serious writing, Mark?"

"What I do!"

"What you did is done. What people did in the fifties, and sixties, and seventies, and eighties, and nineties, is done. It is the same as the movies. It is blockbuster time."

"Yes, but … not you. Your house is not like that."

Now Ryan was not only angry and disgusted, he was animated. He banged his coffee cup down and shouted over the table.

"You are taking up my valuable time!"

"This is my time. I have an appointment with you."

"Do you want me to spell it out for you, Mark? Didn't you notice the workmen in the lobby … what they were doing?"

"No."

"Salter and Salter Publishing has been sold."

"Sold?"

After the shock settled a bit, Mark asked, "Who bought it? Don't tell me you are going in with …"

Ryan, letting his emotion subside, just shrugged.

"No, no, no. One publishing company doesn't buy out another these days. The situation is nothing as simple as that. We are all being gobbled up into a vast corporate pyramid. We are not separate from other business interests per se. Who are the new owners? I cannot even get a clear picture of that myself. I do know that a Dutch outfit will have direct business dealings with our offices, yet the Dutch connection is a wholly owned subsidiary of a German based firm that that has global interests and not just in publishing … we are small potatoes for them … but deal in armament, textiles, lumber, retail … and … do you get it now? It *is* the bottom line that counts, Mark. You do not contribute to the bottom line. Why don't you accept that?"

"But you said that I was to come with outlines so that …"

"Mark. I have another meeting in two minutes. Don't make yourself over into someone pathetic."

"Am I being dumped from your author list?"

That was too much. Ryan pushed a button and barked into the intercom.

"Tell Mr. Sweeny I will be right along."

He started to get up, but hesitated, then said this to Mark.

"We gave you fair warning. If you insist on sticking your head in the ground like an ostrich then that is your affair. Now, if you do not mind I really have other business."

Mark, as angry as he was naïve, countered with the only card left in his deck.

"Listen to me. I am with it. I am. My fiancé is about to get her doctorate in literature and she intends to be a literary agent and as soon as we are married she is going to take over directing me and soon enough I will be properly represented when approaching the publishing world and so you … I don't care what you call yourself these days … you better not dump me because I am … my fiancé can make me … hot."

Hearing this Ryan barked out a laugh. He got up from his chair, came around the desk looking taller than Ryan remembered, grasped the novelist by the back of his elbow, lifted him out of his chair, and firmly walked him towards the door of the office. As they walked, he spoke softly in Mark's ear.

"You are one of a kind, Mark. You are so out of it there can be only two reactions to you. Either we get angry or we laugh. Your fiancé is getting her doctorate in literature? She is going to make you hot? Know that the publishing world is chock full of ambitious young woman, all armed with doctorates in English Literature, and all of them coming to these canyons thinking, believing, imagining they can change the shrinking literary market. You know what happens to them? Most of them go home with nothing. The rest, the ones who come aboard, end up working for peanuts. They end up bringing me coffee. They end up reading scripts we never will publish. Not in a hundred years. Not even if you put a gun to our heads. They end up crushed. They end up conforming. One out of fifty lasts until she is thirty. The rest go off to some non-New York place and have babies. Good luck to you, Forrest. Good luck to you and your determined fiancé. Now … I must go."

Chapter Nine

Mark stood up at straight as he could and with his belly tucked in so that his spine arched, but still a handful of sharp needles from the pine tree stuck him in the back causing him to wince and reminding him of Slattery in the crepe restaurant. He couldn't move forward or backward. His apartment had not been this crowded since a night, ten years earlier, when Carrie had used his place for a women's "break the glass ceiling" affair. He had stayed through that to serve hors d'oeuvres and to be made the butt of some rather nasty jokes by young ladies who took him to be the token white male corporate president holding them all back.

"Your attention, please!"

The crowd did not respond, and for a moment he thought he was going to be forced another step backward so that the tree, already listing with too many ornaments, and with a shaky stand that kept dripping water onto his carpet, would tip over. He decided to yell.

"Hey! Hey!"

Friendly catcalls greeted this. Finally Mark resorted to struggling a few feet to his left, climbing up onto an arm of one of his old couches upon which four people were seated and with four more plopped on their laps. Weaving dangerously, Mark pleaded, "People! I want to give a toast."

More catcalls, then an almost reverent silence was granted him.

"First of all, we are here to celebrate Christmas, which, and contrary to rumors as to its demise, is still alive and well and being observed here on the upper eastside with generous dollops of joy."

A chorus of boos met this mild opener; jokes were not Mark's strong point; public speaking was not his forte. Unworried, he pressed on.

"Secondly, we are here to congratulate …"

Expectant roars drowned out his voice out. He overcame this by shouting.

"To congratulate Jill Cartwright for successfully completing her doctorate in English Literature!"

The cheering was wild. No surprise there. The majority of the people in the room were graduate students at N. Y. U. Yet there were as well, and much to the novelist's chagrin, a good many people who did not seem to belong in his apartment but had gotten in anyway, this being the holiday season with lots of floating parties going on in his building and on his floor.

People raised their glasses and craned their necks trying to spot Jill, though no one did. At that moment she was bent over and moving through the crowd towards Mark. She gained the place where he was and wrapped her arms around his thighs. Mark looked down at the top of her head. Jill was sporting a shiny, spiky hairdo these days, one that made her look a part of the Hip-Hop generation. The novelist gave her head a pat and the crowd cheered the more. Finally Mark continued his toast.

"And three … we are here to announce … Jill and I are here to announce … that we are not only engaged to be married but that the wedding day is set for March first."

Some people clapped, some cheered, some raised eyebrows. No matter the reaction they made sure they kept drinking. It was impossible to get to the bar set up in the kitchen, so bottles of vodka and gin were being passed overhead, along with two large dripping ice buckets. Mark, helped down to the floor by Jill, took her in his arms and they stayed where they were because they could not move. No one could move. All over the room, people talked to whomever was nearby, and most of that talk was split between the topics of Jill the Ph.D. and Jill the pending bride. The frankest comments, blessedly, did not reach the ears of the loving couple. One knot of Jill's "friends" were firing off a volley of quick comments.

"She didn't get the job."

"Oh, you mean the one at Columbia?"

"They hired a woman from Stanford who has ten years experience and who was willing to take a pay cut."

"She was bummed out about it, I hear."

"Well, Jesus, born today by the way, what did she expect? The world is so full of Ph.D.'s in English, and all from good schools, that a lot of them are thinking of turning them in for subway tokens. I mean, do the math."

"Oh, you are a riot of originality. Don't worry about Jill; she'll hook on. It takes time."

"You know she just flew in from one of those meat markets?"

"Beg your pardon?"

"One of those job fairs. I hear she *was* offered a starting job in south central Iowa or some God-forsaken place like that, but she turned it down."

"Who can blame her?"

"Yes, but that is how you start. You don't start right off here in the big city; you start in some cow pasture and write your way back."

"Why didn't she take the job, then?"

"You know why."

"Oh. Him! I suppose he wouldn't move to Iowa."

"He's the one making the money. He can't leave."

"How old you figure him for?"

"He's sixty. I heard that from this someone who knows his nurse."

"He is *not* sixty. That man is not a day over fifty-nine."

"Nothing changes. They can talk all they want about older women and younger men but when you look around the men are as old and as dirty as they ever were."

"I hear he doesn't make much money."

"Judging by this dump I think you may be right. Have you noticed the furniture here? The guy is clueless. You'd think this was Branson, Missouri for God's sake."

"He doesn't bother with trappings. He's a writer."

"I thought he was a doctor."

"He's a doctor that writes."

"He ought to be one that operates. Then we could have had this thing catered and get to sit on decent couches."

"So Jill is going to marry a man more than twice her age. Is she really going to teach? I mean if she ever finds a job."

"I hear she wants to push his books."

"I never even read his books. Did you?"

"No."

"No."

"No."

"No."

The crowd thinned a bit by nine in the evening: there was another N. Y. U. event scheduled downtown and then another, and yet another. After that there were as many additional events scheduled as one cared to attend. Those who stayed at Mark's apartment could now move about like human beings. Now able to meet their responsibilities as host and hostess, Mark and Jill separated and mingled individually with guests who were drunk on their feet and swaying dangerously.

Jill talked to fellow grad students about her career plans, drawing them as vaguely as she could. As she moved along one wall a large middle-aged woman confronted her, holding a glass of gin in each fist. This person greeted her as if warning her of something dreadful.

"I'm Sol's wife."

"Ah … all right. Hi."

"Sol said you aren't hiding out in grad school any more. What are you going to do with yourself now?"

"I will be speaking to some literary agencies after the holidays."

"You have a book you wrote?"

"No … not … about work. About working for them. About becoming an agent."

"I thought you were a teacher."

"I am trained in … I am not a teacher. I *may* teach but … I really want to do both."

"Why don't you teach for the city? They could always use another teacher."

"City College? I didn't apply there because …"

"No, I mean teach in the city. God knows the kids today are all hoodlums but once you get in the union the pay is guaranteed. Sol says it's the biggest rip off since welfare."

"Excuse me … I think I see someone I know."

"Go right ahead," the large woman said, raising her fisted fortifications. "But if you do take my advice, stick to primary school kids. They can't beat you up as readily unless they come on in waves."

Mark, working his way down the opposite wall, ran into a man who was grinning knowingly.

"Hi, I'm Carter."

"Hello, Carter. Mark Forrest. Are you, ah, finding everything you need?"

"Oh, yeah, yeah. I just wanted to talk to you."

Carter was at least fifty. He was wearing an ill-fitting tweed sport coat that would not close over his potbelly and his hair managed to be both short and unkempt.

"About what?"

"You're the novelist, right?"

"I write novels, yes."

"Good, you will know what I am about then. I work for the City. I'm in licenses and inspections. It's not bad. The mayor's office leaves us alone and we are mostly not stressed out. We have free time to do what we want on City time if you get me. Anyway, I have been thinking about putting some of that time to good use."

"More inspections?"

Carter looked at Mark as if he was an idiot.

"No, no. I have been thinking about writing a novel for about fifteen years now."

"The same novel?"

"Well it only takes one to hit, right?"

"So they say."

"I have this idea that what is going to be the next best seller is to do with terrorism."

"That is a topic of conversation all right."

"You agree with me, then?"

"Well … there are novel subjects, and then there are tabloid headlines."

"What do you mean?"

"That the people reading the headlines do not read novels."

"I don't buy that."

"Well …"

"Listen. I want to ask your help on this novel I am going to write. What do you say?"

Mark just stared at the man but that did not stop him.

"I figure you have to have violent characters stuck in the book if you are going to write about terrorists. I mean I can … I guess I can sketch in the outlines but … as far as … you know … adding the little tricks and such … the way to turn a sentence and all … I mean could you look at … or advise me on … I am not asking you to actually write in the sentences but … I mean unless you are interested … but if you could …"

"Excuse me, host duties call."

As Mark moved away from Carter the man called out to him.

"Look, I don't mean to … you know how it is. Everyone is writing a novel these days so as to pad the old c.v. I mean it is a pain in the ass but you have to do it!"

Mark missed hooking up again with Jill as they both headed for the window on the short wall, for she was corralled that moment by a group of undergraduate students whom she had served as a teaching assistant. Instead of grasping his fiancé he grabbed a passing bottle instead, and after pouring himself four fingers of vodka, turned his back to the party and stared out his window at the street far below.

There was not much of a view. Every time he looked out this same window he made this same remark.

"It is not much of an apartment, either."

There was no question of moving. He couldn't afford it, plus it was convenient and then some to his work. Besides, this *was* the upper eastside; he must never let himself forget that. He was surviving quite nicely compared to others.

He sipped his drink, fighting back a rising bitterness. These last six months, from that meeting back in June with Ryan Salter till now, were mixed. There was Jill, thank God. He loved her. He was going to marry her, though it was not until very recently that he saw clearly what it meant to marry her. She did not have an independent income like Carrie did, at least not yet; they would be living quite modestly for the foreseeable future and, unlike Carrie, who had transformed her independence into a religion, Jill had abandoned her studio at N. Y. U. immediately upon defending her thesis and had moved in with him. He was working longer hours downstairs to make ends meet. He and Jill were becoming a New York couple who did not fit the definition of one, and yet he liked that; he no longer felt the loneliness and the emptiness and the incompleteness that had gnawed at him when he was sleeping in one bed and Carrie in another bed in another apartment in another part of the city.

The new gal Friday he had hired to take Janie's place was efficient, but did not once volunteer to stay the extra hours to help him through his paper work; as an employer he could find no specific fault with her but still, losing Janie the way he did gave him the feeling he had been left in the lurch all these months. Then there was the fact that he had no one to sit down with on those dark afternoons when he lost a patient to cancer or to some other terrible suffering. Janie had been strong during those times; she had been there for him during those times. There were so many of his patients died this fall alone. Johanna Murphy died just that week. It had torn him up inside more than he expected.

As for Ryan, Mark's eyes narrowed and his fingers closed so tightly on his glass he finally had to let up before he broke it. He had gone on writing, of course, for he was a serious novelist, but here the bitterness was at its worst and was not going to be stifled by any argument.

"I think back to the years when the walls would move, when I was learning my craft. There were no guarantees then as now. I knew the odds were against me, but I thought that if I did not burn all my bridges common sense would hold me back. I settled for the work one must do. So who am I to complain about a surface called literary success?"

More bitterly still, Mark centered on exactly what his aesthetic life had come to of late.

"Nothing has changed down deep. I write the same as I always did. I love it. I am good at it. I am just plain good. I have no right to feel sorry for myself if I am not a Jerry Stevens. I mean, how can I be both a good, serious writer and a best seller, too? Ah. Jill says that can be done. She names the names. I can't deny what she says."

Sipping vodka, and still keeping his back to his remaining guests, he assessed his talent redundantly.

"I can write. I am elite."

He said this with self-conscious petulance reverberating in his brain. It forced him to add, "Yet I am an elitist in my own designated place."

"Mark? You OK? Merry Christmas!"

He turned around and smiled.

"Hi, Marty. Hi, Janie."

A handshake from Marty and a formal hug from Janie were followed up with more greetings of the season, plus the expected congratulations. Standing there like a molting blond bear, Marty's large arm completely encircled Janie, who had finally cut her bushy hair and now looked like an earnest woman with squirrel-like features. The three of them ran out of things to say and were embarrassed. Marty reached for another cliché.

"How does it go?"

"A good night for Jill."

Marty, who was afraid to act hail and hearty seeing Mark was so obviously down, used this excuse to open up a little.

"Yeah! We spoke to her when we came in. Sorry for being so late. Janie wouldn't let me leave the hospital until I had looked at every record pertaining to my patients this month. Plus I happened to pull Christmas duty this year."

"He has a lot to learn about efficiency," Janie piped up with a gleam in her eye.

Janie had quit working for Mark in September, giving him only a week's notice, and had taken a job with the hospital Marty was attached to, and started dating him in mid-October. They had announced their engagement Thanksgiving weekend and of course Marty had taken Mark out to tell him the news.

"Janie's a wonderful girl, Mark."

"Yeah, I know."

Once this was over with, Marty got drunk and ended up moaning the loss of his freedom once again. Mark had voiced his understanding while rolling his eyes the while.

"The thing is, Mark, Janie talks about medicine and … never a word about my writing."

"Yeah.'

Once she had the ring on her finger Janie felt comfortable seeing Mark socially; she even suggested double dates, but Jill did not go for it.

"Thank God," Mark thought at the time.

Within the hour everyone left the party but a few of Jill's closest friends, young woman who sat on the floor smoking cigarettes and running their hands through their long hair. They turned to talk about novels and novelists, never once mentioning Mark or any of his books. They said things like:

"That guy from Texas? The one who writes about raw-boned cowboys? *He* can write. I mean sometimes you are just starving to pick up a book from someone who can really, really write, and he can really write."

"I know what you mean. I mean … you walk around this city thinking … where are the novelists who can write?"

"It is not easy."

"I know. I mean there is the Texan and …"

"That is about it."

Jill seated herself with the girls so Mark went into the kitchen to start cleaning up. His dishwasher was filled and in mid-cycle, so he began washing glasses by hand at the sink. He wore a smile on his face, one that made him look his age had anyone been looking at him. For some reason he began thinking of the Foss.

She had gotten his ten thousand dollars to do publicity on his third novel and he had found out, this week, that he had sold nearly a thousand copies of *Bleak* during this latest six-month inventory. The royalties he would get from Salter and Salter would not quite cover the Foss investment but he had no right to complain: he had more readers than before and he had received a dozen fan letters. These letters were all alike in that all twelve fans wanted to know when his next book would be coming out.

"I would like to know that myself."

Mark had settled on the script he wanted to get published next. It was a sequel to Slattery's adventures in the aesthetic realm and he entitled it *Bleaker.* Jill, practicing to be an agent, publicist, literary critic, set up a reading of his script in an independent bookstore in the Village and they had gone there last Thursday evening.

The bookstore was called "The V." Mark never heard of it but Jill heard it was popular and arranged the reading over the telephone with the owner, a woman named Joe.

When they arrived by taxi and walked through the door Mark's first thought was that they turn around and walk out again but Jill wouldn't hear of it.

"This is how you start, Mark. Now go ahead."

It was a Lesbian bookstore and coffee shop. Besides the owner, Joe, there were three women seated at one table and all three had their backs to the raised platform where Mark was to read. Politely enough, the women turned half way around in their seats when he introduced himself.

"Hi," one of them mouthed.

He read the passage in his novel-script, *Bleaker,* where Slattery, some ten years older than he was in the novel *Bleak,* returns to Scottsdale, Arizona to try to catch a second look at the landscape behind the mall, the one that had opened up the secrets of aesthetics to him.

"It wasn't there. What was there was another mall."

Mark read the whole passage but stopped well short of his intended twenty minutes. The three women stared politely, and when they clapped they did it so discretely, so that Mark could see their hands moving but could not hear the sound. Jill stepped up on the platform next holding copies of his three published novels and announced that these were available at discount prices. The women smiled and turned their backs. When they left the place minutes later neither he nor Jill could say who was the more embarrassed.

It was getting on to two-thirty in the morning before the cleanup was complete and the last guests left the apartment. Mark was exhausted. He had to be up in less than three hours to get ready to write and he had a full schedule of patients to see after that.

They stumbled into bed and Jill rested her head on Mark's chest. She was well aware of his darkening mood now, and she was worried about him, but she could not think of what to say that might help. Of late she was beginning not to reach toward his down moods; she realized they came as regularly as phases of the moon. Yet as Mark was drifting off she did think of something to say to him.

"Don't despair, Slattery. Look how many doctors were famous and serious writers. Chekhov, Maugham, ah …"

"Celine."

"And the poet, ah, from Paterson there, across the river?"

"William Carlos Williams. Right."

"Well, there you go. That's a start."

Avon, Connecticut, December 2nd, 2004

www.ingramcontent.com/pod-product-compliance
Ingram Content Group UK Ltd.
Pitfield, Milton Keynes, MK11 3LW, UK
UKHW041928190726
13854UKWH00004B/1514